ANGELUS ICHOR

ANGELUS ICHOR

Hans Graf

SAINT DUNSTAN'S PRESS

BALTIMORE, MARYLAND

Copyright © 2020 by Hans Graf.

All rights reserved. No part of this publication may be reproduced, distributed or transmitted in any form or by any means, including photocopying, recording, or other electronic or mechanical methods, without the prior written permission of the publisher, except in the case of brief quotations embodied in critical reviews and certain other noncommercial uses permitted by copyright law. For permission requests, write to the publisher, addressed "Attention: Permissions Coordinator," at the address below.

Saint Dunstan's Press
612 ST. Dunstan's Road
Baltimore, MD 21212
http://www.saintdunstanspress.com

Publisher's Note: This is a work of fiction. Names, characters, places, and incidents are a product of the author's imagination. Locales and public names are sometimes used for atmospheric purposes. Any resemblance to actual people, living or dead, or to businesses, companies, events, institutions, or locales is completely coincidental.

Book Layout ©2020 David Haber

Cover Art ©2020 Hans Graf

Angelus Ichor / Hans Graf. -- 1st ed.
ISBN 978-0-9963237-6-5 (epub)
ISBN 978-0-9963237-5-8 (paperback)

CONTENTS

HIM	1
HER	11
HERE	19
FREE	33
WITNESS	39
LIE	47
AFTER	55
TRAP	63
SEARCH	73
CONFRONT	79
GONE	87
CONSOLE	93
RESPECT	103
DISBELIEF	111
IMAGE	119

TORMENT	125
REVELATION	139
OBSERVE	151
RETURN	163

In our continuous movement toward learning, we can be inspired by everything around us. No one thing is insignificant. This story is dedicated to those simple connections in a complex world; family and friends.

Most notably, Martha Graf, Elsa Graf, Adam Bridge, and Dave Haber.

Your support, inspiration, and overall friendship contribute to this beautiful world.

Be wary of the objects you worship. Turn towards the world you were given and the companionship of others to truly find Peace.

HIM

Pavlo stood at the Wall of Remembrance running his hand down the stone face. He occasionally stopped his fingers at an engraved name.

"We must live on regardless of the past," came a voice from his left.

Pavlo remained facing the wall and spoke, "and find peace in the present"

He turned and faced the voice. It was Vera, *Councilor of the Environment*. She carried a satchel that held her various tools. The two smiled and each held up an open hand.

"Welcome to the Fane, Pavlo."

It was spring, the time to share ideas, goods, and news. Pavlo left his village late that morning after tending the garden.

His village was one of many that was located within the valley. Together they formed a collective. Each village was tailored to its natural surroundings and was connected by a network of paths. At the center was the Fane, the place of sharing and the home of *The Council*. Vera was one of the four members.

"Our spring onions turned out well, thanks to your advice, Vera," Pavlo said graciously. "We started our main planting this morning."

"Glad to hear. Your timing is good considering the moisture level."

Pavlo shook his head in agreement and said, "The blossoms are in full bloom and so vibrant." He turned to look at the valley. Vera joined in his observation.

Pavlo was fond of the valley in which the Fane was nestled. Glaciers formed it long ago. The ice had pushed the earth's surface into folds that ran parallel and defined its edges. The land between was temperate and fertile. Spring water trickled down the slopes to form a small river that flowed east to west. Wetlands lay periodically in the lower lands, helping in times of floods. To the north, meadows of wild grasses and flowers flourished on the high ground. Broad leaf trees lined the edges of the open spaces and slowly transformed to pines toward the upper ridges. Each habitat was home to small mammals, birds, and insects. This world was an enriched place of biodiversity and an ecological paradise.

"Well Pavlo," Vera said, "I must attend to our group session. You are more than welcome to come join us." Each *Councilor* would host a meeting to facilitate interactions amongst the various villages. It provided the right atmosphere to share ideas.

"Thank you for the offer, but I have other matters to attend to. Oanna has requested my presence, but if time permits." He paused and smiled. They both turned toward the Fane. Vera waved and then left for a small group forming at the southern Pavilions.

Pavlo breathed in the fresh air and watched the gathering of the others. The villagers had come to the Fane to share in their bounty. It brought balance and stability to their daily lives. Most importantly, it promoted community and built strong bonds.

The Fane was the culmination of their society. Though simple in form, it was well-composed. At the north was the Wall of Remembrance, to the south the Pavilions, to the west the Grotto.

Pavlo returned to the Wall to collect his belongings. He had left his satchel and straw hat at the base of the structure. The wall was roughly seven feet high and a hundred paces long. It was made of stacked stones slightly larger than the average hand, each engraved with a name of a villager whom was no longer living. At the head of the wall was a small platform with three steps leading up. Services for the living and the deceased were given here. Beyond and to the west was open ground preserved for future generations. The wall retained an earthen mound planted with a line of Cyprus trees. The tree spacing maintained the peaceful rhythm of the valley, framing the sky and landscape beyond, a reflection of the present and future.

Near the platform of the wall was *The Councilor of the Built Environment*, known to all as Luca. He had a table set out before him that held a variety of tools, paper, and drawing utensils. Leaning over the table, he was engaged in conversation with a villager while others encircled them to closely observe. Their discussion was focused and fulfilling. Villagers were encouraged to solve problems. Key to their communication was the ability to draw and prototype ideas.

Pavlo put on his straw hat to protect his face from the peaking sun. A young girl from his village had given it to him as a present, and he wore it well. He was a man of calm stature with an average build. He was jovial, good natured, thoughtful, and always approachable. He slung his satchel over his shoulder. It held the essentials, a container of water, some dried fruits, and a small utility tool.

At the center of the Fane was a large flat open space used for the Exchange. The ground was covered with gravel. Its outer edge was lined with small stones that were smooth and round, each carefully placed by hand.

Pavlo walked to the middle of the Fane to meet with the other villagers. They had parked their hand carts around the perimeter to display their bounty. He moved from group to group giving and receiving greetings.

Pavlo strolled the southern edge. It was lined with open air pavilions with thatched roofs. Large deciduous trees were rooted to provide shade in the summer months. The natural spring water of the Grotto fed the outlying vegetation of the Fane and the westerly wind created an inviting atmosphere.

Under a large shade tree, a group was learning new stretching techniques from *The Councilor of Body*, known to all as Ramund. He promoted health and wellness through preventative actions. Good fitness contributed to a happier life.

Pavlo came to the Grotto and entered. The air was fresh and cool.

The Grotto lay nestled at the mouth of a large rocky mound; it formed the head of the Fane. Stone carvings decorated the concave surfaces. At the lower level were vignettes depicting pain and suffering. These were the stories of the past. As the viewer ascended so did the message. Groups of figures entwined in natural beauty covered the ceiling. This was the world they knew and loved.

At the center lay a small pool of water. It was fed from a spring that trickled from a small crack in the stone face. The water basin was amorphous in shape and overflowed through a carved scupper in a low wall; this was the life source of the Fane. The low wall was a place of rest for those who visited, its width and height designed as a bench.

Inside was a group enjoying a story accompanied by two musicians. Bursts of laughter radiated from the space as the orator preformed. Joy and warmth filled the air. To the far left Pavlo spotted *The Councilor of the Mind* standing by herself. He approached and greeted her.

"Oanna, it is good to see you again." He held up his open hand. It was customary to address *The Councilor* by name. She held up her hand in return and smiled. She was an unimposing woman with a friendly disposition. Speaking with her was comfortable and filled you with optimism. The two were familiar with one another from past interactions. She spoke.

"I am pleased that you have come upon *The Council*'s request. I need you to help me with someone."

Her statement intrigued Pavlo; he was always one for giving support. It was not an unusual request.

"Please continue," he said cordially inviting her to share more.

"A boy has been brought to my attention. His life has been guided in doses and his adaptation to our philosophies are in question. We are requesting ..." She paused and adjusted her words to give Pavlo the choice. "We are asking to place him in your care. It is our belief that you can guide him best ... To help him find his way. We do have other options if you wish to be free of our request." She smiled at Pavlo after saying these last words.

Oanna and *The Council* were experts in these matters, and their recommendation of Pavlo was flattering. He immediately responded.

"How could I refuse if you say the boy needs my help?"

"You have chosen well, Pavlo. We can expect good results. Please wait here while I get the boy." She turned toward her shelter. On the south side of the Grotto was a small path. It curved along the rocky surface, flanked by wild shrubs. The trail led to a modest shelter where *The Council* resided. There was a small garden terraced into the mound of the Grotto below.

Pavlo enjoyed watching the villagers while he waited. He could hear bits of their conversations and it filled his mind with good thoughts. He cared deeply for the people of the collective. It filled him with serenity.

Oanna was gone momentarily, returning with the boy. He was in his early teens, almost a man. His hair was slightly long and a bit unkempt. He stood straight with his shoulders held back exaggerating his chest; his face showed confidence. He carried a bag strapped over his left shoulder..

"Pavlo, this is Marius." Oanna placed her hand on Marius's back bringing him forward. Pavlo offered his hand. "It is a pleasure to make your acquaintance. It appears that we will be spending a great deal of time with each other."

Marius reached out and clutched Pavlo's hand. He had a strong grip for a boy of his age. As they shook hands, Pavlo was struck by the boy's eyes. It was not the color that he was taken with, it was their depth. His gaze was hollow, without end.

"As well," Marius replied.

Their hands separated as did their eyes. Pavlo turned his attention to *The Councilor* of Mind.

"If there is no further need ..." Pavlo paused for a moment giving Oanna a chance to respond. Her posture and smile was his answer. "Then, it was a pleasure to see you again."

There was no exchange between Marius and Oanna as the three of them stood in the Grotto. The silence was awkward and impersonal. The Musicians from storytelling rescued the moment as their harmony interjected. Pavlo used this as his cue for their departure. He playfully bowed and waved his hand motioning Marius. "Shall we?"

Marius stepped forward without reaction to Pavlo's silly gesture. As they walked from Oanna, she said, "Peace to you, Pavlo."

HER

They left the Fane and headed west toward the village. Marius followed. He initially held back until Pavlo adjusted his stride to keep them side-by-side. There was little exchange of words during their walk. Pavlo tried several times to initiate a conversation giving Marius the opportunity to speak. He chose to remain quiet. Silence it was.

Pavlo pointed out the sites. They saw the wetlands to the south and several unique trees along the riverbed. They observed the stone-faced ridge in the distance.

"From up there, you can see the whole valley," Pavlo described with enthusiasm.

Marius took notice in silence.

The river valley became wider and they could see a windmill as it popped up above a field of grain. Pavlo smiled as he could see his village ahead. He was delighted to be back home. The path wandered between the grain to the north and a field of hemp to the south. Two stone piers marked the threshold to the village. Pavlo stopped just outside of the gate.

"Welcome to your new home, Marius. I am sure you will find everything that you need here, especially companionship. Let us get you settled, and then I will give you a tour of the entire village." Marius lowered his head with a quick nod of approval. They both passed through the gateway and continued on the path.

Ahead they could see the thatched roof of the central hall. The large structure was surrounded by a fence with a garden on its southside. The vegetable plants were arranged in close rows with direct access to the central hall. Several of the villagers were out for *Contribute Time*, each at their work. Pavlo waved to those that noticed their arrival and received a cordial wave in return.

They continued on the path that led them into a stone plaza to the north of the great hall. They entered the courtyard. From the space, a crescent shape formed by the adjacent shelters was easily recognizable. Each house faced inwards toward the central hall.

They left the courtyard heading west until they reached the last shelter of the crescent.

Farther to the west sat two larger buildings; these were the various shops. Pavlo and Marius walked past the central hall and headed toward them. As they approached, Pavlo guided them to the shelter adjacent to the shops.

"Here it is, your new home," Pavlo said while stepping onto the porch. Marius remained out front to observe his new residence.

The shelter was typical of the village. It had a large stone wall that faced south. The thermal mass helped keep the shelter's temperature consistent. The roof sloped in one direction away from the large wall and was thatched with natural reeds from the valley. At the front, the roof over hung to shade a small porch. Next to the front door was a large window.

"The village uses this as our guest quarters. We occasionally have helpers for larger undertakings. There are no visitors in the near future, so it is all yours to explore."

Pavlo stepped aside and gestured for Marius to open the door. "Freshen up and make yourself comfortable. I will be back in a bit to give you the full tour."

Marius stepped onto the porch and reached for the handle. He looked pleased with his new arrangements as he moved into the shelter. Pavlo smiled and left the porch.

Marius went to the middle of the domain and stood. He slowly rotated to observe the details of his new home. The main space was cozy, with a small room in the back. The ceiling followed the roof line so that it was high and open. There was a ladder near the door that lead up to a small loft containing two beds. A large window in the loft let natural light filter through the entire space. The shelter was slightly larger than the typical villager's, as it was for visitors. On the main level were two beds both tucked against the stone wall. The outer walls were made of wood and contained two windows facing a side garden. There was a wooden table with four chairs between the windows. The shelter was simple and had all of the essentials for its guests.

On the far end was a counter with a sink and lower cabinets. Neatly stacked bowls and dishes sat on a set of open shelves above. To the left of the kitchenette was an open door to a bathroom. Natural light filtered in through a high frosted window.

Marius decided to take the bed closest to the bathroom on the main floor. It had a wooden dresser that was to the right. He took off his pack and set it on the bed. He went to the dresser, slid open each drawer, and looked in to make sure they were empty. He then opened his pack and systematically removed the contents onto the bed, sorting each item in an orderly fashion. He refolded his clothes and stacked them neatly before putting them into the drawers. Two small pouches remained near the pillow. He picked one up and went into the bathroom; it contained items he needed to freshen up. He washed his hands and face and then returned to the main space leaving the pouch behind.

Marius stood still for a moment and scanned the shelter a second time. He stepped toward the bed and picked up the remaining pouch. It was sealed with a long draw string, allowing him to loop it over one shoulder. With freed hands and obsessive eyes, he started his systematic search. He opened all of the cabinets and drawers of the kitchenette noting their contents. He looked through each dresser and checked all of the beds. Any space that was enclosed, he investigated until he had meticulously explored the entire shelter. His search came to an end when he found a loose wall panel near the table. He worked his fingers behind it to reveal a gap. It was perfect.

He took off the pouch and slid it into its new home.

"What are you looking for?"

Marius immediately straightened, but calmly turned around. He faced a young girl. She was standing in the threshold of the front door. Her hair was like a mop, thick and curly, and she had bright eyes. She was at the edge of adolescence, being a few years younger than Marius, and much smaller. She spoke again.

"I hope I did not startle you. I saw you through the window as you were looking around, and thought you might have lost something. So ... I came in to see if I could help. Hi, I am Daphne."

She waved her hand and smiled. Marius was reluctant at first and then smiled back. He moved toward the table and placed his hand onto the surface. Slowly rubbing the top as he spoke.

"I haven't lost anything. I was just studying this table." He glided around it as his hand remained in contact with the surface. "I admire its craft. Do you know who made this?"

She came in and sat down in one of the chairs. "That is funny," she chuckled. "Because I saw you fiddling with the wall when I came in ... as for the table, I do not know who made this. Most of the furniture is made in our shop or traded at the Fane. Have you seen the Maker Shop yet? I could take you there if you like." She was animated while she talked and Marius was becoming annoyed. He walked over to the bed and she gleefully followed him. Her excitement increased as her curiosity grew.

"You have not told me your name?"

"I'm Marius."

"Well Marius, how did you get here?"

"I came here from the Fane with my mentor Pavlo."

"I like Pavlo. He helps my father, Oscar, in the Maker Shop. My mother is Sonia and she likes to help at the Mill." Her chatter picked up again. Marius stretched out across the bed and put his hands behind his head.

"This must be where you are staying. When visitors come, they use this shelter and the one next to it. I like it when visitors come."

"If you don't mind, I would like to be alone."

She found his statement strange. "How silly you are! Are you not a bit curious of your new home and of the people here? I would be delighted." With joy, she started to hop from foot to foot while throwing her hands outward. She hummed a tune and spun around. "Maybe we could play later?"

"Maybe," Marius said softly to himself.

Daphne skipped to the doorway and grabbed the handle. As she closed the door, she smiled and said, "Byyyye Mariusssss."

He was alone again .

HERE

Marius stood by the window looking out over the garden. He observed villagers strolling along the river. It was late in the afternoon and the morning work was done. It was now *Free Time*. He saw Pavlo making his way toward the shelter. Under his arm was a stack of books. He stepped onto the porch and knocked. Marius let him in.

"These are for you. I thought it would be good to review the basics." There were four books total, each pertaining to *The Council* divisions. He placed the books on the table. "Besides this reading, I would recommend you take up a musical instrument. It is good for the soul as well as the mind. You can find more books and instruments in our Main Hall." He paused and looked around. "I see you have unpacked and chosen your bed. It looks like you are all settled in... well then, shall I show you around?"

Marius nodded yes and out the door they went.

"Let us start with what is close and do a full circle." They walked west toward two large structures. The buildings were staggered with the southern one projected forward. On the ends were large open sliding doors. Marius followed Pavlo into the first building

"This is our Maker Shop. We use it for repairs and fabrication of needed items." There was a long work bench to one side and multiple machines to the other. A variety of hand tools were hung on the walls. Everything was well organized and maintained. At the back were shelves lined with materials. A man approached carrying boards under his left arm. He was large and muscular with broad shoulders. His face lit up with joy as he saw the two of them.

"Hey Pavlo," he said as he came toward them. "Who is the young man with you?"

"This is Marius. *The Council* requested he come to our village." Pavlo stood to the side allowing the man to address Marius.

"It is a pleasure to have you. I am Oscar." He reached out his right hand and they shook. Marius took notice of Oscar's large calloused hands, his skin toughened from years of working.

"Daphne mentioned you."

Oscar laughed at Marius' response. His laugh was deep and infectious. It took Marius by surprise. Pavlo could not help but chuckle.

Oscar composed himself and spoke.

"It does not surprise me that you have talked with her. Very curious she is." He set the boards onto the work bench and noticed Marius scanning of the Maker Shop. "Do you like tools?"

With a hint of arrogance, Marius clarified, "I like making things."

Pavlo remained positive, recognizing Marius's interest in the Maker Shop. It was the first time he saw the boy show any excitement, so he made a suggestion to the both of them. "Maybe you could help Oscar during *Contribute Time*."

The sly smile on Marius's face showed his approval of the suggestion and Oscar responded, "I am sure we could find something for him to work on."

Oscar was friendly and open to giving opportunities. His appearance was a bit gruff, but deep within, he was a gentle giant.

"Great!" Pavlo paused looking to Marius. "Well, shall we continue with our tour?"

"Talk soon," Oscar said as he picked up the boards and returned to the back of the Maker Shop

They departed through a side door.

Marius was excited as they left and Pavlo was grateful for Oscar's friendship. It gave hope for Marius to find a place to fit in and feel comfortable.

They entered the space between the two buildings. It was modest in width and partially covered. It contained a furnace, a kiln, and racks of tanks to one side. To the other side were shelves of material that sat under the overhanging roof.

"This is where we make glass, pottery, and forge metals. The tanks hold gases captured from our bioremediation system. We will tour that later."

Fresh air from a pond in the backed cooled the courtyard. They exited toward the waterway. They came to a channel lead upstream from a small dam. The raceway directed water to a turbine that powered the two buildings.

They passed the channel by crossing a small wood bridge. Beyond was the river and forest. They returned to the front of the second large building and looked in through the sliding door.

"This is our Trade Shop, it is where we make fabric, soap, oils, and other products from our hemp crop. You may have noticed the plants as we came through the front gateway." They went inside. It was laid out similar to the Maker Shop. Along one side was a line that displayed the clothes that were made. They were hung up to air dry. On the opposite side were canisters of natural dyes and a long work bench. The Trade Shop was unoccupied as they looked around.

They left and headed east toward the vegetable gardens. Around the perimeter was a row of brush and to the inside was a woven fence of thickets. It was about two feet high and kept small animals out. They entered through a gate and strolled about.

"The arrangement of our garden utilizes the natural pesticides of plants. We worked closely with Vera, *The Councilor* of Environment, to establish this layout. Companion planting provides us with the most yield using the least amount of land. We had an aphid problem recently, so we added this row of cilantro."

Pavlo bent down and looked at the surrounding plants. "It looks like it is working well." He was delighted by the results while Marius remained still faced.

They exited through the east gate and crossed over the main path of the village. In the distance, a wind tower perched over the field of grains. At its base was a stone building with two large cylinders used to store their yield.

"This is our mill. We use it to grind grain, press fruit, and make oils." Pavlo directed Marius to have a look. They peeked inside to see the machinery. A slender woman with long braided hair was pulling a wooden lever attached to a press. She applied force slowly, evenly.

Their eyes caught each other. She immediately stopped and came over. Pavlo addressed her with good spirits.

"Sonia, I would like you to meet Marius."

"Well, I knew you were headed to the Fane, but did not expect this surprise." Genuine warmth flowed with her greeting. Marius' attempted smile revealed his favoring of her.

"Daphne described you well," she said as she looked him over. "I am pleased to welcome you to our village."

She leaned to one side placing her right hand on her hip. Her head tilted with her invitation, "Now, if you need anything, come see me... okay?" She smiled in a humorous and caring way.

Marius nodded and smiled back at her. She lowered her arm and moved back to the press.

"But... as you can see, I need to finish a few things before *Gathering Time*. We can talk more later." She smiled and placed her hand on the press lever. Pavlo respected her request and the two of them left the Mill.

Once outside, they circled to the back to see the green house. It was long with a directional roof. In front of the structure was a patio. They walked to the center to find a cast iron lid embedded in the stone surface. Pavlo placed his feet to either side of it and bent down. He stuck his fingers into the molded hand holes and lifted. Gently he placed it on the ground. Marius was intrigued by what was inside and moved in close for a better view. "This vault is our cistern and is the first stage of our bioremediation system. All of our used water is piped here. It is the first link in a chain of containers. The rest are inside the green house." Marius got on his hands and knees to peer inside. Pavlo waited for him to finish his inspection before resetting the metal lid. He rubbed his hands together to brush off the flakes of dirt. His actions inspired Marius to brush dirt from his knees and hands.

Dusted off and partially cleaned, they went into the green house. As Pavlo described, the structure contained a series of large tanks, each filled with a variety of plants. Above the space was a line of oscillating ceiling fans. Their spinning kept the air circulating and helped the process of purifying the water. Pavlo walked over to the second tank and put his hands into the water. He fished around and pulled up a small pump.

"Last week, our nitrogen levels were higher than usual. Luca, *The Councilor of the Built Environment,* came and helped us solve the issue. This pump was malfunctioning, so Oscar and I repaired it."

Pavlo held the pump with both hands as he described the situation. He took pride in what the villagers could accomplish, but his display was humble. He submerged the pump back into the tank.

They walked the length of the green house, exiting through the back. Once outside, Pavlo turned to look up at the towering windmill. The sun was bright as he lifted his hand above his eyes to protect his vision. Marius mimicked him as they both looked at the spinning blades.

"This wind tower provides the power for the majority of the village, but the primary purpose is for the Mill and pumps."

Behind the green house was the final stage of the bioremediation system. The largest of the containers was a pond. It was covered with lily pads and other water plants. They walked the outer edge until reaching the north portion.

Pavlo cautioned Marius, "Try not to make any sudden movements and remain calm. I want to show you our bee hive."

Near the edge of the pond was a wooded arching structure. It had a glass front that allowed you to see the inner workings of the hives. On the sides were panels that could be opened.

Pavlo looked closely through the glass, admiring the fascinating creatures. Marius shared in his curiosity and peered closely.

"Honey bees are essential to our way of life and should be treated well. They pollinate the plants that provide our food. Their honey is a natural sweetener and alleviates allergies. Without insects, we would cease to exist."

Together they listened to the buzzing of nature's music.

Adjacent to the pond was the Orchard. It buffered the village from the northern winds. Pavlo and Marius ventured in.

There was a variety of fruit trees; pears, apples, cherries, and peaches. In the center of the orchard was a clearing for all types of wild berries and grape vines. At the southern end were the nut and olive trees. They stopped at the clearing to have a quick taste.

The two left the clearing and headed to the edge of the orchard. It was lined by the backs of the shelters. Each building had a small outdoor space facing the trees. They passed between two shelters. Each structure had a porch that shaded the entrances. The shelters were similar in shape and size, almost identical.

Upon closer look, the details became personalized. Subtle differences, such as wood carvings and ornate patterns gave each shelter its own identity.

Pavlo guided them to a porch, "I thought you better know where I reside."

They both stepped into the outdoor enclosure. Marius noticed a wooden owl perched above threshold. The front door opened and a women stepped out. She and Pavlo embraced quickly as Marius watched.

"Lydia, I would like to introduce you to Marius."

She graciously went to Marius and gave him a welcoming hug. He remained withdrawn, but displayed a forced smile as they separated.

"I am glad you are here. Pavlo and I will do our best to make you comfortable."

The boy remained smiling with no other response. The silence was awkward causing Pavlo to speak.

"It is getting close to *Gathering Time* and I think we better head to the Main Hall. Would you like to walk with us, Lydia?"

She accepted Pavlo's offer reaching out her hand. The three of them left the porch and walked to the Main Hall. It was the largest structure of the village, with an ornate thatched gabled roof. The long sides were clad with wood siding and vertical lattice. Several types of vines grew within the frames, blooming in multiple colored flowers. The gabled ends had large doors and glazing above to let light into the vaulted space. The doors were open and you could hear the villagers inside. Pavlo stopped at the entrance courtyard and spoke.

"This is our Main Hall and gathering space. We meet here in the evenings to eat and socialize. It is the heart of our village." He pointed to the features. "Notice the four cylinders. They are for ice storage. Below this courtyard is a grid of geothermal wells. Energy is all around us, but it is up to us to use it wisely. What we choose to take, we must return or else we will be destined for failure."

Pavlo's words were directed at Marius as advice for all of life's decisions. He placed his hand on the boy's shoulder to lead him into the Main Hall. Lydia followed.

At the entrance were three rows of connected tables, parallel to the room. To one side were the service spaces, closets, and restrooms. On the opposite side was a large opening that displayed the kitchen. Past the tables was an open space for villagers to stand or dance. Beyond that was a raised floor used as a stage. Daylight filled the room from the glass of the gabled ends.

The villagers huddled in an array of activities. The cooking group was preparing to serve while others relaxed and enjoyed each other's company. Pavlo lead Marius to the stage, while Lydia made her way to a table.

To the left of the stage sat a bell. Pavlo lifted a mallet that hung next to it. With one swing, he struck it and the room became silent. He had their attention. Pavlo's voice projected throughout the great space.

"All, I would like to formally introduce you to Marius." He extended his right arm with an open hand toward the boy. "*The Council* has placed him in our care as he journeys to manhood. Please welcome him to his new home."

He escorted Marius from the stage as the villagers came to greet him. It was time to eat and socialize.

FREE

The spring was replaced with the warm air of summer. Pavlo helped Marius establish a routine. They scheduled a rotation of activities during *Contribute Time*. To start the week, he and Pavlo reviewed past lessons and set goals. Marius' time was divided up between the Maker Shop, the garden, and the bioremediation house. These activities occupied the majority of his day. During *Free Time*, he would take solitude in the woods. He rarely chose to be with the others, especially in groups. Not being able to avoid *Gathering Time*, Marius had to adapt. He observed the others and molded his interactions to fit in and become familiar with everyone in the village.

Pavlo was in the orchard checking on an olive tree that had signs of Peacock spot. He was on a ladder making close observation of the leaves.

"What's the verdict?" Oscar was at the foot of the ladder. He held a mint leaf in his hand and raised it to his nose to smell. Refreshed by the scent, he moved the leaf to his mouth and clinched down on it with his teeth.

"It is bit early to tell, but I think we resolved the winter spotting. It was good that we added nitrogen to our compost for the base of the tree. It seems to be working. We probably should ask Vera for her opinion. She would be able to confirm if it worked." Pavlo climbed down from the ladder as Oscar held it steady. "What brings you out to the orchard? I thought you were helping in the Trade Shop today."

"I was ..." Oscar paused and looked over his shoulder. "I need to talk to you about something that has been on my mind."

Pavlo faced Oscar, they had been friends for a long time and it was rare for him to show a serious side. He knew it had to be important. "Please tell."

"I left the Maker Shop yesterday after cleaning it up. You know me, I try to keep the place organized. Well ... when I returned this morning, I noticed a few things missing. At first, I thought maybe I forgot to put the items back, so I looked around the Maker Shop. I could not find what was missing." He took the mint leaf from his mouth and dropped it to the ground.

"A hammer, a container of nails, some twine, a board, and a ... a knife." He paused. "I thought maybe someone had borrowed them. Usually when things are taken, the person leaves a note on the chart as a courtesy. I reasoned that they must have forgotten ... no big deal. But it was the missing board that stuck with me."

"What was special about it?" Pavlo asked.

"It was a simple board with no unusual markings. What is strange is someone went out of their way to have that specific board." Oscar's hand shook up and down punctuating his last words.

Pavlo's forehead wrinkled as he tried to decipher Oscar's meaning. "I do not understand..."

Oscar filled in the gap. "You see ... there is a whole shop full of boards separated and stacked on the back shelves as inventory. If someone took one of those, I would have never noticed it missing. The board I am talking about, I was planning on using today. I placed it in a lower drawer of the work bench. It is an unusual place for me to put boards... but we all have our quirks." He smiled and a short breath of air blew out his nostrils recognizing his faults. "The reason I am telling you this is... I think Marius took everything."

Pavlo remained calm regarding Oscar's accusation. He wanted to know more. "What makes you think this?"

Oscar took a deep breath. "He was in the Maker Shop when I put the board in the drawer, and I know he saw me do it. I remember him staring at me as I stood up. You know how he does that?" Pavlo acknowledged with a nod, and Oscar continued.

"He has his own quirks, but I have not had any trouble with him ... until this incident. When he came to the Maker Shop today, I asked him if he had seen the missing hammer. He said no. I believed him, at least until I opened the lower drawer. Not seeing the board and remembering how he stared when I put it there... That is when I knew he had lied to me. I chose not to confront him on this issue, lying is no light matter. It goes against our teachings. Lies can compound into serious destructive behavior if not handled properly. We all know to come to you if we have any issues with Marius, so I have."

Oscar's posture loosened as the words left his mouth and mind, the weight had been lifted. Pavlo recognized his friend's relief and placed his hand on Oscar's shoulder.

"I appreciate you bringing this to my attention. I will do my best to remedy this issue with Marius."

The fragrance of the orchard refreshed the two men. There was no need for further discussion. Oscar concluded with a practical point.

"As for the missing items, there is no rush on their return, we have spares ... Thanks for listening." They shook hands and Oscar headed back to the Maker Shop to finish his repairs.

WITNESS

The morning was warm; it had been weeks since the items went missing. Pavlo and Oscar had not spoken of the incident since the occurrence. The two men were hard at work in the Maker Shop repairing a treadle pump that was needed for the irrigation system. The spring planting was done and midsummer was a time for watering. Luca, *The Councilor of the Built Environment*, had given sound advice to Oscar regarding the foot pump, and it was important to make it operational. Pavlo gave assistance as the two worked most of the morning during *Contribute Time*.

"I can finish it up. Thanks for the extra hand." Oscar enjoyed working with Pavlo and was genuine in his gratitude.

"It will be great to see it functioning again. It could not be better timing." Pavlo spoke with satisfaction. "I guess I will go wash up."

"It should be good to install tomorrow. Until then." Oscar put up an open hand as a friendly gesture.

Pavlo returned it. "Until then."

He left the Maker Shop and headed for his shelter. He walked across the village and enjoyed seeing everyone along his short trip. The day was bright. He reached the door to his shelter, opened it, and stepped in. Lydia was at the far end of the room pacing. She stopped upon hearing the door and turned to face Pavlo. Her complexion was pale and her hands were shaking.

He knew something was wrong as soon as he saw her. Her appearance and behavior was highly unusual; he was immediately concerned.

"Lydia... what is the —"

She rushed to him with her arms open. She wrapped herself around him and he around her. His hug provided the comfort she needed without knowing why.

They stood quietly.

Lydia finally let her arms down cluing Pavlo that she was ready to talk. His arms slid to her hands. They moved to the small table near the window and sat.

"I need to tell you something that is disturbing," she started. "But first I must start from the beginning."

Pavlo sat patiently. "You have my ears and my mind."

She took a breath and began. "Three weeks ago, I witnessed Marius playing near the woods. It was afternoon *Free Time*. I never really noticed him there before. He had a few sticks and some string and was working on something. I did not know what it was, and at the time, I had no concern. I treated the situation like I would have with any of the other children his age. There was no sense of harm, and I considered it his own curiosity or project. A few days had passed and from just random luck, I saw him again ... working as before. I kept a distance with the idea that he needed space, but I chose to watch him. I could not help notice the vigor at which he worked. His mind was focused on his project. He was absorbed. He stood for a moment and wiped his brow and that is when our eyes met. We were locked in. His face was devoid of feeling. I do not remember how long we looked at one another. It felt like an hour. Then he slowly curled his lips to form a smile. His smile drew out the coldness of his eyes, a sight that gave me chills... I was frightened."

Lydia paused and looked into Pavlo's eyes; she squeezed his hands and continued.

"I have never felt that. I have always been surrounded by love, friendship, and the sense of security. Everyone in our community helps and cares for one another. It is our way. It is what we have been taught as well as what we have taught others. It is our balance with the world... I felt none of this in that moment with him.

"I turned away and left, unable to continue my observations. I tried to remove him from my mind by thinking of others to distract me, but I could not. The moment stuck with me even as I tried to hide it away. I do not want to think poorly of Marius. I only want what is best for him. I truly did and still do."

She looked out the window and gazed at the garden. She was struggling to remain positive especially with the rest of her testimony. She had to push through.

"The next day, my curiosity got the best of me, and I consciously returned to the edge of the woods. Marius was not there, and his project was gone. I did a quick scan, but saw nothing. So my feelings subsided and I returned to my routine.

"For the week to follow, everything was normal. I had several interactions with Marius, and he was perfectly fine. I never received his smile again, and I started to recover from what I thought may have been a misunderstanding, but I was wrong in my assumptions.

"Yesterday I saw Marius in the same spot by the edge of the woods. This time he was entering into the forest. I stopped and watch him as he stepped from the high grass into the shade and then disappeared. I froze ... and my mind returned to his cold smile. My curiosity was bursting and my heart began to burn. I waited a few minutes and then walked to where he entered. I could not help myself, I had to follow.

"I stepped into the shade of the forest, the coolness was refreshing, but also chilling to my mind. I have never been afraid of the woods. I have always respected it, but have never feared it. In reality, it was not the woods I feared. It was Marius. I could not see him so I moved forward. I proceeded slowly with caution so that I would not be heard. I must have gone about a 100 paces when I finally caught a glimpse of him. I saw the red of his shirt through the green of the woods. He was in a small clearing, kneeling down over something. I kept my distance and memorized the location by observing the trees. I only stayed long enough to be sure I could return, and with that I left.

"*Free Time* was nearing *Gathering Time*. I helped the others and did the evening routine. I inquired of Marius' activities for *Contribute Time* with Sonia and knew that he would be occupied in the Mill the next morning. So I woke up, prepared our morning needs and found the time to return to the woods."

Lydia paused for a moment. Pavlo remained still and patient. His eyes were wide and attentive and his mouth held shut. His teeth were pressing tight as he waited.

"This time not concerned with caution, I moved quickly to where Marius had been kneeling. As I approached, I saw his project. He had built a trap of some kind. I had never seen anything like it. Sticks were lashed together to form a cage. It was coned shaped at one end with an open hole. The end had a ring of sharpened sticks facing the opposite direction, I guess to keep any creatures from escaping. It was about four feet long. I do not think it was his first attempt considering the craftsmanship. It was in a small crevice and camouflaged with leaves. If I did not memorize the location, I may have missed it. I looked inside the trap and it was empty.

"I stood tall, took a breath and then noticed a second project. About 10 paces away there was a board. It was hued like those from the Maker Shop. It was leaning against a tree so I walked over to it. I turned it over and almost fell down in fright. A small animal had been nailed to the surface."

Pavlo's hands let go of Lydia's and covered his mouth. His eyes were blank as he stared in disbelief at Lydia.

"I am not done," Lydia whispered. "The animal was alive."

LIE

"You would not believe the horror unless you saw it with your own eyes," Lydia said. "Just speaking of it deeply disturbs me."

Pavlo removed his hands form his face and returned them to Lydia's hands to comfort her. "Are you sure that it was alive?"

"When I first turned the board over I was startled by just the site. Its limbs were stretched out and each appendage was carefully fasted to the board. The head was tied with twine to nails on either side. It was a small raccoon."

She paused, closed her eyes, and whispered to herself. "Oh that poor creature! Its fur was sliced and pealed back revealing its internal organs. How methodical of Marius. Its skin was pinned in small increments, and as I was observing ..." She held back her tears. "That's when it started its long loll of a whine. How could he do that to a living creature?" she punctuated as her torso started to flutter.

Pavlo knelt from his seat and slid toward her. His arms encompassed her as her head rested on his shoulder.

"I did not know what to do. I wanted to end its suffering, but I could not get myself to do it." She sobbed and then added, "If I did, Marius would know that someone had found his experiment. The only thing I could think was to find you. So I turned the board back over and leaned it as before, wishing the animal peace. I hurried back here trying not to be noticed by anyone and waited for you."

Pavlo tightened his hug and then released. He slid back to his chair looked her in the eyes and said, "I know that this memory will be with you, and I hope that time ... and I ... can bring you comfort." He paused. "What you have told me is deeply disturbing. It goes against the teachings and threatens our place in the world. To act this way toward other species is a serious matter."

He thought for a moment and then stood up, "I do not doubt any of the things you have told me... I will need to see this for myself. We must have more than one witness. This issue will need to be raised with *The Council*. I will not subject you to this horror again. Do you think you can describe how to get there?"

Lydia was positive as she gave him a full description.

Pavlo left the shelter and headed to the woods. He walked with conviction; fortunately he did not have any encounters on his way. He made it to the edge and entered into the woods. Lydia's directions were simple to follow and he made it to the small clearing.

He found the crevice but there was no trap. He noticed the disturbed ground where someone had swiped the dirt. Leaves were spread in an unnatural way. He looked for the board and that was gone as well. He thought hard about the possibilities. Marius must have returned and cleaned everything up. How did he know or was it just luck? Did he see Lydia in the woods?

Pavlo thought to himself, could Lydia's story be untrue or somehow mistaken? He knew it was wrong to question that possibility. She would never lie to him. They had a life together and shared the same beliefs. He knew her as she did him; they were close enough to read each other's thoughts. He was so assured of her truth that he never questioned it.

What now?

He returned to the shelter to find Lydia sitting in meditation. She was concentrating on breathing to calm her thoughts. Before she could ask, he said, "Everything was gone."

"Are you sure you were in the right spot?"

"Your directions were accurate. This I know to be true. The evidence was gone, but there were traces of clean up all around. The ground had been swept and was dressed to cover any trace of misconduct." He was frustrated by not finding anything.

"What are we to do? I know what I saw and we need to do something to address this."

Pavlo was unsure of the decision that needed to be made. He had never felt frozen before, especially while mentoring. His instincts and conditioning had served him well in the past, but this was beyond anything he had experienced.

"I will address the issue with him, as well as inform *The Council*. I assure you of this, but I will need time to think of the best approach. We should act as usual for the time being, as hard as that may be."

Lydia was unsure of his tactic, but she knew that Oanna had given him the responsibility of Marius. It was his obligation so she honored his advice.

The evening came quickly and it was time to gather for eating. Pavlo and Lydia went to the Main Hall as always. Marius was in the kitchen area helping Sonia. They were preparing asparagus with mushrooms, dressed in olive oil and rosemary.

The hall was set with three long wooden family style tables, flanked on both sides with wooden chairs. The villagers took their seats as the food was brought out. Pavlo and Lydia choose to sit at the far end of a table. Oscar and Daphne strolled over and joined them.

After serving, Marius and Sonia came and sat beside them. Dinner was normal; the conversation was light and friendly. Oscar talked of the treadle pump and their success so far. Sonia was complimentary to Marius for being helpful with dinner. Daphne, as usual, told of her day. Pavlo and Lydia remained quiet and attentive. The food had been passed and their appetites filled. It was then that Marius chose to speak.

"There is something I need to tell all of you. It is a dilemma I experienced today. It is of the troubling sort, and I do ask for your sympathy."

It was an unexpected address to the group and Pavlo and Lydia were caught off guard. Maruis leaned in and faced everyone. He wanted to make sure that all could hear, and then he began his story.

"I was in the woods today during *Free Time*. It is an activity I enjoy. The woods bring me happiness most times, except for t-t-t-t-t-oday." A stutter cut his speech. He gathered himself with a deep breath. "You see... I... I found an injured raccoon in a small clearing. It must have fallen from a tree; for it was impaled on a stick. I was horrified by the sight. It was so bloody and gruesome." He exaggerated the last words while shaking his head.

"The dilemma being that it was still alive. I could tell by the noises it was making. My stomach knotted up as my throat became dry. I didn't know what to do. It was in so much pain. I know it is wrong to kill animals, but I wanted to give it mercy... mercy from its pain. So I did... I killed it. Was it wrong? I beg you, was it?" he burst out in tears and lowered his head to rest on his folded arms below.

Sonia was the first to react. She was sitting next to Marius and immediately leaned over him and started to rub the back of his neck. "You poor young man. What a horrible thing to have happen. It is over now. Everything will be okay. It will."

Oscar was the next to console. "I do believe that under the circumstance you acted with dignity. Showing mercy to any suffering creature would be forgivable by us and *The Council*." Oscar turned to Pavlo. "Would you agree?"

Pavlo sat with his lips slightly ajar. He face was blank. Marius had just lied to everyone and was believed. How manipulative and calculating this act was. He underestimated Marius' abilities. He looked at Lydia and sensed that she felt the same. He remained silent. In shock.

"Would you agree?" Oscar repeated with a look of confusion.

"In truth I would have to," he said softly.

Marius' crying subsided after a short while. He finally lifted his head and sadly said, "If you don't mind, I think I would like to return to my shelter."

"A bit of rest would serve you well," Sonia said with sympathy. "Leave your plate, and I will take care of it."

As Marius left the table, he glanced at Lydia; there was no smile this time. It was a quick look and telling; he was victorious for the moment.

AFTER

The end of summer came with all of its pleasantries, the warm sun and longer daylight. The valley was in full green glory. It was *Free Time* and many of the villagers were swimming in the pond by the Trade Shop.

Daphne was weaving a straw hat. She had decided to make a replica of the one she had made for Pavlo. She was planning it as a gift for Marius. The two of them had been working together for several months now, and she thought it would be funny that the Mentor and Mentee have matching hats. She worked that morning on it. Upon completion, she ventured to Marius' shelter to give it to him. The door was cracked open when she arrived.

"Marius? What are you doing?" she asked as she stood outside the door. There was no answer. She peeped her head in. Marius was not in sight, so she went in to make sure he was not hiding from her. Past experience had made Daphne aware of his tricks to avoid her. She checked the bathroom and the loft with no luck. He was nowhere to be found.

She placed the hat on his bed and went to the table to find paper and pencil to leave him a note. From the corner of her eye, she noticed the wall panel near the table was ajar. Her memory flashed back to the first day that she met Marius, and his peculiar behavior around the paneling. Her curiosity got the best of her, as she looked around for possible witnesses. She went over to the panel and placed her small fingers in the crack. It moved easily and revealed a pouch hidden within. She hesitated, thinking that it was not right to sneak through other peoples things. Upon further thought to herself... maybe just a peak.

She reached in and removed the pouch. It was closed with a draw string neatly tied at the top. Pulling the string, she untied it. She inserted her index fingers in and opened it wide. Inside were a dozen white objects that she was unable to identify. She reached in and pulled one of them out. She held the object up in the light and closely observed it.

It was the skull of a small mammal. Daphne had never seen one of these and at first glance was unsure of what it was. She rotated it in her hands to see all of it. Turning it upside down, she peered into the base of the skull with one eye closed.

"What are you doing?" burst an authoritative voice. Startled, she put the skull back into the poach.

"Nothing."

She turned around and Marius stood in the doorway. His hands were at his side with his elbows bent. He appeared to be blocking the door. Daphne knew she was wrong and after her initial reaction confessed.

"I came to bring you a gift and noticed the wood panel ajar, and when I tried to fix it, it came open." This part was an exaggeration, but from the look she was getting from Marius she felt compelled to protect herself. "I saw the pouch and was curious to see what was inside."

She got up and skipped over to his bed, trying to lessen the tension between them. She picked up the hat and held it out to him. "I made this gift for you. It is just like Pavlo's. Do you like it?"

Marius stood like a statue, cold and emotionless. He stared at her as she waited for his response. She tried to remain calm as he gazed at her. Daphne felt compelled to try again to diffuse the situation.

"Well if you do not like it, I could make another one for you. Maybe you could help?"

His demeanor shifted with her offer as he diverted his stare toward the table. "No need. I like the one you made."

"Here, let us see if it fits." She approached him with the hat and reached up to place atop his head. He leaned forward as she reached. He stood up and used both hands to adjust it while walking toward the bathroom mirror. Daphne stood still and watched for his reaction. Marius looked from the corner of his eye while facing the mirror. He could see her eagerness. He made a second adjustment and pivoted his head.

"It's perfect," he said coming back into the room. He went to the wood panel and removed the pouch. He reached into it and began taking each skull out and placing them on the table. There were twenty-one in all. He set the pouch to the side and started to rearrange their order. When he was finished he knelt down to get eye level to the table and looked each one over.

Daphne remained still while watching his ritual unfold. As he knelt, she slowly worked her way toward him. "Are those what I think they are?" She paused. "Skulls?"

"You are correct."

"Well... where did you get them?"

"I found them in the woods. Every day at *Free Time* I search for them. I have learned to follow large birds to their nests. This has been the best way to find them." Marius was filled with pride.

"Why do you like them?"

"Come here and see." Marius encouraged her to come closer. She knelt down beside him and looked as he did. He spoke in a quiet voice, "When I look at them, I can see their faces as if they were still alive."

He picked one up and held it in front of his face. "This one, I imagine, had a patch of dark fur on its left cheek." His description made Daphne uncomfortable. She stood up and turned toward the bed.

"Well I think the whole thing is a bit strange. My father told me to never play with wild animals. I think that means even dead ones. I wonder what he would say about this."

Marius became agitated by her suggestion and quickly began putting the remains back into the pouch. "You're just like all the others. I knew you wouldn't understand."

She sensed his frustration and empathized, "Understand what?"

"I think if you went into the woods with me you would see what I mean. You may realize why I am interested in these things." His voice was coaxing as he attempted to lure her. "But, you mustn't tell anyone. As I said, they wouldn't understand."

She hesitated. "I am not sure... you know it is not good to keep secrets."

"Don't think of it as a secret, think of it as a lesson. It could be our way to learn about the world. Why can't we do this free of elders? You made this hat on your own, didn't you?"

"Of course I did. I make a lot of things on my own."

"See, you are independent."

"I guess..." Daphne was still unsure.

"It's settled, then. We'll go tomorrow at *Free Time*." He spoke with conviction as to not let Daphne change her mind. He put the pouch back behind the panel, and as he sealed it shut, he put his index figure to his lips. "Shhhhh."

He escorted her to the door. "Now if you don't mind, I have something to take care of."

She was relieved to be on her way. Her innocence was replaced with unease. She quickly left his shelter and went to the garden. When she reached the gate, she turned and saw Marius stepping from the porch. He headed toward the Maker Shop. He wore his new hat. Her unease dissipated. She could not resist smiling. She watched him stride on until he disappeared into the woods.

TRAP

***Contribute Time* for Daphne and Marius occurred** as usual. She was helping at the Mill while he was at the Maker Shop. They both had lunch in the Main Hall but did not converse. Their eyes met many times while they ate with the other villagers. Daphne was the first to shy away from their exchanges. When lunch and cleanup was finished, they both left the Hall. Marius followed her on the way out. She walked fast toward the Maker Shop only to be intercepted by his faster stride.

"You're not backing out of our expedition are you?" he mocked.

"No, I was just going to get a few items." She spoke quickly.

"I have everything you'll need." He nodded his head while smiling. His gesture gave her an uneasy feeling. "But ... if you insist, go on and get whatever you think you need and meet me at my shelter. Hurry up though, we don't want to be gone too long."

Daphne moved quickly to the Maker Shop. She was unsure why she went there; she just wanted a moment by herself. A part of her was reluctant to go on Marius' expedition. It was not fear; it was his erratic behavior that did not sit well. If she decided not to go, he would badger her. She did not want that. By going, she could always back out of future expeditions based on the outcome of this one.

It was this logic that convinced her to go. Now that she was committed, what did she need to take? She looked all around the Maker Shop. She scanned the tools until her eye caught a glimpse of a small saw blade. It was about five inches long and was used to cut patterns in wood. It had leather wrapped around one end as a handle.

Daphne did not know why she chose the blade; it just seemed to be the right thing. She lifted her pant leg and slid it into her sock. As with any item from the Maker Shop, she went over to the board near the main work bench and signed it out. She left the Maker Shop for Marius's shelter.

He was inside putting his pack together. When she entered, he closed it and put it over his shoulder.

"Did you find what you need?" he asked sarcastically.

Daphne smiled and did not answer his question. She instead changed the subject. "Well, are we going?" she inquired with a hint of silliness. Marius brushed past her out the door. He turned and beckoned her to follow.

They walked quickly past the Maker Shop to the edge of the woods. Daphne followed closely as they moved beyond the village. They pushed into the woods under the canopy of the trees. Shaded from the sun, it was cooler as they rustled through the leaves of Falls' past. They did not speak. Daphne had been in this part of the woods and was familiar with the surroundings.

As they travelled further, Daphne broke the silence. "I do not think we should go any farther from the village."

Marius stopped and opened his pack to take out a flask of water. He handed it to Daphne.

"Let's rest a moment and have some water," he suggested.

She took a drink and handed it back.

"I have searched this area before without success. Where we need to go is much further and worth it. We need to go where the large birds live. I know you are strong enough to make the trip and will love my surprise."

His words sparked Daphne's curiosity

"Surprise, what do you mean?"

"If I tell you, it will spoil the excitement."

Daphne could not suppress her delight. It added just what she needed to move on.

"Okay, I am ready when you are," she said with enthusiasm. The two pushed on.

They came to a clearing at the base of a rocky ravine after walking for more than an hour. Marius' excitement grew, reflecting his own glee.

"Your surprise is just around this outcrop of rocks. Why don't you take the lead so you can see first?" He let her pass him as Daphne's interest peaked. Her gait was at full stride as she rounded the corner.

Her surprise was revealed.

Lined in tight vertical rows were wooden stakes driven into the ground. A series of horizontal rings rose from the bottom to the top every eight inches. The structure was no taller than five feet and five feet in diameter. Daphne stopped and stared at the frame wondering what is was.

Suddenly she was grabbed, her arms pinned, and pushed forward. Startled and off balance, she was lifted and crammed against the enclosure. She began pushing back, but could not get any leverage. She was forced downward through a small opening at the side. Her head and shoulders scraped against the wooden frame. She began kicking frantically. His weight prevented her movement. She felt twine slip over her right wrist and her arm being pulled down. Her second hand was grabbed and clasp to the other. Tied tight she was pushed once more and lay stomach down captive in his cage.

Daphne rolled over to face the opening and Marius. He was kneeling down at the entrance facing her. In his right hand, he clasp the knife he had taken from the Maker Shop.

"Now, you're going to do what I tell you to." His eyes were dark and focused.

She froze.

Their glance was short lived as he reached his left hand for a pile of sticks to the side of the structure. The knife remained between them, ready to strike. Daphne heard the buzz of a wasp as it flew into the enclosure. Her fear of Marius subsided by the insect's presence. She calmed knowing that stillness would prevent her from being stung. The wasp flew to the top of the cage and landed. Crawling on the frame, it remained between her and Marius. He was too busy to notice as he wove with one hand the branches, covering the entrance. Finishing, he lowered the knife and opened his satchel. He pulled out some twine and began lashing together the newly placed pieces.

"Why are you doing this to me?" Daphne said with a quiet tone.

"You shouldn't have snooped through my things. I know you were going to tell the others about the skulls, and I can't have that."

"I was not going to say anything and I will not say anything now. Just please let me out, please!"

Marius worked vigorously as he pulled the twine tightly. He snapped back. "You're right about that. You won't tell anyone anything because you're not going to see anyone. I control your fate!"

Tears began to slide down Daphne's face as she begged. "Please let me out! Please! Please!"

"Go ahead and cry. It won't do you any good. It's just the two of us out here."

Daphne slipped her bound hands around her knees as she sat with her back against the cage. Squeezing her legs, she lowered her head and sobbed. It was her only comfort in her time of shock. As she cried, her mind calmed. She collected herself. Could she reason with him?

"Why are you doing this to me? I have only been kind to you. I made that hat for you as a gift of friendship. Are we not friends?"

Marius was unaffected by her words. The response he gave was immediate, as if he had always known the answer.

"You gave me this to mock me! Thinking I am like Pavlo. I will never be like him. He is weak and incompetent! I will deal with him in due time."

Daphne remained steady, even with his harsh thoughts. "You are so wrong. Pavlo is caring and giving. He has only shown you love, just like the others in the village. How can you not see or feel this?"

"They are all weak and pathetic! They need someone like me to take control. They are all sheep in need of a Shepherd. I am just fulfilling my destiny." Marius picked up the knife and held it up. He stared at the blade to see his own reflection. "You see, Daphne, I had to put you in this cage. Loss is the best way to inspire change. Crisis truly change people, and this is just the beginning."

Marius completed lashing and reinforcing of the cage. He stood up and grabbed his satchel. He put the knife into the bag and took out his flask. The water ran down his throat as he drank it empty. Now refreshed, he rubbed the back of his hand on his lips removing the moist residue. He slung the bag over his shoulder.

"Well, it looks like my work here is done. I better be on my way; for, it is going to get dark soon."

The thought of nightfall rushed into Daphne's mind as she pleaded, "Please do not leave me here alone! Please do not ... please."

"You better get used to your new shelter. I've other matters to attend to. Don't miss me while I am gone." He leaned over placing his hands on his crafted cage. "Oh ... I shall return ... try and prepare yourself for what is to come."

He lifted his hat and wiped his forehead with his forearm. He placed it back on his head, took a few steps, and was gone.

Daphne sat alone in the cage.

SEARCH

Pavlo and Lydia entered the Main Hall for *Gathering Time*. They helped set the tables for dinner as the others filed in. Most of the villagers had arrived and were doing their part as usual. Lydia sat down while Pavlo finished his conversation with a small group. The children were washing their hands after being outside.

Pavlo made his way to where Lydia was sitting and sat across from her. He saw Oscar approaching with a peculiar look on his face. He had known Oscar long enough and could tell when something was wrong.

"Have you seen Daphne? It is unlike her to be late for *Gathering Time*." As he asked them, he scanned the room for her. "Sonja is checking the village."

"Last I saw her she was leaving the Hall with Marius at the beginning of *Free Time*," Lydia spoke up.

Pavlo immediately searched the Hall for Marius. The two of them were missing.

"Come Oscar. Let's make an announcement." The two men went to the front of the Main Hall and proceeded to ring the bell. The sound brought everyone to attention. Pavlo spoke.

"Have any of you seen Daphne or Marius? They are unaccounted for. Please share if you have." A couple of the villagers approached the two men offering to help with a possible search. But no one had any information. The villagers decided to postpone *Gathering Time*, a large number of villagers exited the Hall to check the grounds. They organized into small groups to cover more area. Pavlo and Lydia checked the orchard.

They moved quickly and remained focused. Lydia was the first to show her concerns.

"This is unsettling, considering Marius's behavior." Her witnessing of his recent activities was vivid in her mind. Pavlo tried to remain positive.

"Daphne is smart for her age. I am sure there is an explanation. They will turn up." He said this to keep Lydia positive and to convince himself. His did not want his mind to enforce his true feelings.

Each villager returned to the main courtyard after their search with the same result. Oscar and Sonja each showed their distress while others tried to comfort them. The light of day was slowly being replaced by dusk.

Marius was spotted running through the main gate. He came up the path into the courtyard. The villagers surrounded him as he tried to catch his breath. Sweat ran down his face as a villager went for water. He spoke frantically as his chest heaved.

"Daphne and I got separated as we hiked the wetlands. I searched and searched but couldn't find her."

"Slow down and catch your breath and start from the beginning." Oscar advised.

Marius took a deep breath.

"Daphne and I decided to go on a hike. The owl above Pavlo's door had inspired me to observe large birds. The wetlands was prime habitat for the species I was interested in. I spoke to Daphne about it, and she wanted to go along. We left at the start of *Free Time*. We went pretty far, which I know is frowned upon, but our curiosity got the best of us. We found a nest and in our excitement Daphne wanted to get a better look. She wandered off as I watched a large bird, and before I knew it, she was gone. I started to panic as I yelled her name over and over ... with no answer. I didn't know what to do ... I ... just didn't know."

His voice cracked and his eyes filled with tears. He grabbed Oscar's arms and pleaded.

"Please forgive me. Please, please ..."

Oscar hugged the boy.

"It is okay. We'll find her. I need you to take me to the last spot you saw her, can you do that?"

"Yes," he replied.

A search party was quickly organized. They collected essential items and reconvened in the courtyard. With Marius as their leader, the group left the village heading toward the wetlands. The majority of the village joined the search. Oscar, Sonja, and Pavlo were at the front of the pack. Lydia remained home as the others left.

The group followed Marius' every step as he led them. It was dark and navigating the wetlands was difficult. They came to the nest that Marius described. It was then that they divided into smaller groups each heading in an array of directions. They agreed to return to the main path by dawn.

They continued the search until early afternoon. Repeating their process of covering as much territory as possible. Their morale sunk with their lack of success. They decided to return to the village and refresh for a second search later that evening.

Pavlo entered his shelter exhausted. He sat down and removed his shoes. The bathroom door was closed when he came in and he assumed Lydia was inside. The door was cracked open.

"Are you alone?" she asked.

"Yes. We were unable to find Daphne. We are going to start a sec ..." He could not finish his sentence as the door opened. Lydia was not alone; Daphne stood at her side.

He was filled with joy upon the sight of her. He got up and came over to hug the girl. She hugged him back. They exited the bathroom to the comfort of the main space. Lydia did not share in Pavlo's joy; she was direct and stern.

"We have a problem," she said.

Pavlo immediately understood the situation from her serious tone. The possibilities of what happened played out in his mind. Lydia's expressions could only mean one thing, and he was filled with dread. Marius was at fault.

Lydia went to the door. "I want you to stay here with Daphne while I go and get Oscar and Sonja. We have a serious matter to discuss with them. I will also inform the rest of the village of Daphne's return. I think it is best that we cancel *Gathering Time* this evening. The search has been strenuous on the village and all are deserving of rest. I will be back soon."

She left the shelter. Daphne and Pavlo sat quietly at the table awaiting her return.

CONFRONT

Marius was lying on his bed with his feet crossed and his arms above his head when Pavlo entered the shelter. It was early morning of the day following the search. Marius was aware of Daphne's return and was instructed by Pavlo to remain in his shelter. The village was quiet as all rested.

Pavlo came in carrying a satchel over his shoulder. Marius remained on the bed as he was addressed.

"You need to pack your things. It has been decided that you are to return to *The Council* at the Fane." His voice was stern and unwavering as Marius sat up.

"When?"

"Now."

Marius was not pleased by the immediacy of the trip. He sat for a moment to take in the circumstances. Pavlo stood still in the middle of the room, watching.

"I am going to need some time to get my things together. I would like to be alone."

"It should not take you long. I will wait." He walked over to the table and sat down facing the boy. His action left Marius pondering, making him move sluggishly. He emptied out his dresser by placing the items onto his bed. He placed his pack near the pillow and arranged everything systematically. He gathered his bathroom pouch and added it to his neatly ordered possessions. He rolled his clothing individually and placed each one into his pack. He was particular of the order leaving his bathroom items for the top. He glanced at the wood panel, but only for a second. He would have to leave his pouch though he felt that was unacceptable. It was his and he wanted it.

"Is that everything?" Pavlo asked

"Yes." He clinched his jaw after the word left his lips. He would have to return for his trophies.

"Alright then. Time to go." Pavlo stood up and gestured for Marius to lead the way. They exited in single file with Pavlo following. They walked across the village to the main courtyard and headed through the gate. There was no talking by either of them. Marius intentionally kept the pace slow. As they came to the edge of the hemp fields, Marius spoke.

"I am going to miss the village, everyone was nice to me. Especially you, Pavlo."

They shuffled along and Pavlo did not respond. They were near the wetlands and Marius stopped, turned, and faced his mentor.

"If I have to go back to Oanna, then I would like to make a last request. I don't know if I will ever see the village again or this valley. My time here was precious, even if you and the others disagree. I would love to have one last look at this beautiful place from up there." He pointed to the open ridge. He continued, "I have never been up there, so I can only image the view. Please Pavlo, I've never asked you for anything before this."

Marius looked sincere in his request. It was true that he had never asked for or demanded anything. It was the one true vice among all of his faults. Pavlo was not sure if he would see the boy again upon returning him to Oanna. It was a simple request, and he acquiesced to his wish.

"It will add time to our travels, but I respect your desire. We can take the trail up ahead."

Marius smiled and thanked Pavlo as he turned around and walked with a faster pace. Relief came to Pavlo. He had been to the ridge many times and it always refreshed his mind. He thought that Marius might find peace there as well.

They followed a small path around the wetlands eventually leading into the woods. The trail inclined at a steady pace as they proceeded upward. They stopped midway. Pavlo recognized Marius' thirst and graciously offered water from his flask. Marius accepted and the two drank. Replenished by the water, they continued on as they came closer to the overlook.

Glimpses of the view snuck between the trees as they thinned out. They traveled parallel to the ridge until they came to the clearing. Marius led the way with excitement and anticipation. He came to the opening and paused with delight. He slid his sack from his shoulder and placed it near his feet without removing his eyes from the vista. They stood side-by-side and stared out over the valley as time stopped.

From atop the ridge the whole valley was visible. The village lay to the west marked by its windmill. Following the river, they could see many of the other villages, along with the Fane to the east. The sky was open and wide, but to the west the clouds were dark.

"It looks like a storm is approaching." Pavlo pointed in the direction. "We should get on our way."

Marius stood still. "I don't want to go back to the Fane, especially to Oanna. She's abusive."

Marius' statement cut. Pavlo remained calm under the weight of his accusation. "In what way?"

Marius was quick to respond.

"When the other *Councilors* are away, she forces me into a small closet. She locks me in for long periods of time and refuses to feed me. She also has poked and prodded me causing discomfort. I don't fight back for fear of what she may do while I sleep. What you don't realizes is how evil she is. She uses her knowledge of the mind to maintain control of me. You think that she is wonderful. It's all a deceitful front. She is sickened."

Pavlo's experience with Marius influenced his reply. "This is a serious accusation you have made. Do you have any proof?"

"I don't need proof; I've lived it."

Pavlo took a moment to process what Marius had told him. The allegations contradicted Pavlo's experience with Oanna. She had always displayed an openness and caring persona; he found Marius's statement hard to believe. Especially with his history of lying. He had witnessed it first hand on several occasions and he was lying yet again. He looked steadily into Marius' eyes to make sure that his words were not misinterpreted.

"I find it hard to believe Oanna is evil, and without proof, you will not convince me otherwise. You have consistently lied, and I believe what you have just told me is false."

"You would side with Oanna because you are just like her. I knew you wouldn't believe me. That's the reason I have to leave the village." He spoke with aggression.

"Your own actions led you to your current standing with the village. You alone stole, lied, tortured, and killed animals. Your final deplorable act was your treatment of Daphne. Her resourcefulness diverted the outcome of your true intentions."

Marius was enraged by Pavlo's statement and started shouting. "Daphne deserved it! She was out to get me! She made up lies, especially about killing those animals. They were dead when I found them!"

Marius' hatred consumed his body in a way that Pavlo had never experienced. In one quick motion, he sprung toward his mentor. His fists flailed in the attack. As Marius lunged, he lost his footing and was gone from sight.

GONE

Pavlo rushed to the edge in shock. Unaware of his position he almost lost his balance. His body instinctively reacted by grabbing hold of a small shrub that kept him from tumbling. Time froze as he peered from the ledge. The decent was more than fifty feet to the tree tops below. His eyes scanned frantically while his body remained still, dormant. Marius was nowhere to be seen.

The distant storm moved swiftly toward the ridge and it began to pour. Pavlo continued to peer, but as the storm strengthened, he moved under the canopy of the nearby pines and started his decent. He moved quickly with assured feet as his mind flashed with disbelief. Conversations formed in his head, each with differing outcomes. Eventually it settled on an endless loop of "he survived the fall... I must help him." The mind trance quickened the journey to the bottom.

"Marius!" Pavlo shouted.

There was no reply.

He shouted repeatedly as he tried to pinpoint the location of the ridge above.

There was no reply

"Marius!"

Each time he shouted, his voice became more frantic. He continued onward with heightened senses. He looked through the canopy to catch views of the ledge. There was no doubt that he was under it now. The storm's intensity decreased into a light drizzle.

He turned to his left and saw it: the cloth of Marius's shirt. He rushed toward him yelling. As he approached, the details of the injuries became clear. There was no need to continue. Marius was dead.

His knees gave out as his adrenaline dropped.

He collapsed to the ravine floor, alone.

A numbness filled his body as he sat. At first there was only the humming of his blank mind, but slowly the world came back. He heard a bird in the distance, calling out. He felt the spots of sunlight oscillating on the skin of his arm as the trees swayed from the winds. Water droplets sparkled as they hung from the ferns around him. The numbness evolved to calm. Time progressed as Pavlo did not.

The calming switched his mind back on and one thought filled it. He knew what he must do. He must take Marius back to the village. As he stood up, a sharp pain throbbed up his right arm. He could not remember injuring it, but somewhere along his decent he must have. It was unimportant to him; he must do the right thing.

Pavlo slowly pulled the body from the brush. He laid it down in a flat area to observe. It was clear that Marius' major injuries were to the head. He checked each limb by gently lifting and twisting. He then removed his outer shirt and gently lifted Marius' head. He slipped the shirt under and folded it neatly over the face whispering, "Peace to you."

Pavlo continued by wrapping the sleeves and loosely tying them below the chin. He placed the arms to the side and fastened them to the belt that Marius wore. He lashed the laces of Marius' shoes together to keep the legs as one. The body was now prepared for the journey back to the village.

He had never been in the ravine and needed to evaluate his best way back. He took a moment to gather his thoughts. As he stood still, the pain of his arm became incessant. It overtook him. He tried to massage it with his left hand with no success. Paralysis set in and he had limited movement of the limb. Pavlo had no recollection of what happened to his arm. He replayed the horrific event in his mind and could form no connection to his pain.

Pavlo refocused on getting back. He gained his bearings and figured out his best path. The most direct route was to ascend back up to the main trail. It was the sure way without roaming endlessly in the ravine. He stood up and moved to the body. He would need to lift him up and over his left shoulder. It was the only way to keep control with the loss of his right arm.

Pavlo gently dragged the body to a nearby tree. He shifted his satchel to his right shoulder to balance the anticipated weight. Then he propped the body against the tree as high as possible and squatted down. In one motion, he placed his left shoulder in the torso and rolled back as he stood. The boy was not heavy, but the lift challenged his physical ability. He remained silent through the exertion.

He was on his feet and started back the way he came. The climb back to the ridge was difficult. He ignored his fatigue and continued onward until he was to the top. Now in familiar territory, he could travel at a steady pace. Carrying the body would add time to his trip to the village. He pushed on through his pain without wavering.

Pavlo neared the village at dusk. The first person to see him was Oscar. He was out checking a fence near the trail head. Even from a distance he understood Pavlo's need for help. He stopped his work immediately and ran to the Maker Shop to get a hand cart. Moments later, he was racing toward Pavlo.

"What happened? Is he alright? Shall I send for *The Councilor of Body*?" Oscar spoke with urgency.

"It was an accident. Marius fell from the ridge… It was an accident," Pavlo's voice cracked. It had been hours since he last spoke. His emotions and physical stress peaked at being back at the village. He was overcome and started to weep.

Oscar took Marius from his shoulder and placed him onto the cart. Instantly, Pavlo fell to the ground. He could finally let go.

CONSOLE

Pavlo awoke in the comfort of his shelter. He could tell it was early morning by the angle of the sunshine streaming through the window. He had been washed and was lying in bed. He could feel the warmth of his sleeping clothes as he slowly opened his eyes. Had he been dreaming? Did Marius really fall? It all seemed cloudy as he came to. As he lay in bed, he could hear a faint exchange of voices but was unclear of the conversation. He gained his bearings and realized the dream was real.

Lydia was standing just outside the door under the roof. She was not alone; a few villagers stopped to check on her and Pavlo. She was gracious but was unable to shake her own thoughts. She turned to check on Pavlo and immediately caught his eyes. They looked at one another, a short glance with a moment of support. Lydia quietly excused herself and came in.

They remained silent as she came toward him. She sat down on the bed, leaned over and embraced him. He lifted his left arm and pulled her closer. They lay in that position for several minutes. There was no questioning, there was no answering, only love.

Pavlo spoke first. "We decided to hike to the ridge."

Lydia sat up to see his face.

"When we reached the overlook, Marius refused to return to Oanna. He tried to convince me by lying about his treatment at the Fane. He continued his avoidance and blamed others for his own actions. Our conversation grew in intensity. I remained calm and firm trying to hold on to our philosophy... our beliefs, *The Council*'s lessons, all of the things that make this world right. He was not accepting and in his anger lashed out at me. In his rage, he lost control... and then he was no more."

Lydia sat and listened.

"I never wanted this to turn out like this. I only wanted to help Marius. Everything I had learned and felt and believed I wanted to share with him. I did not want him to die. He was my responsibility. *The Council* placed him in my care and I failed."

"It was an accident, Pavlo," Lydia said. "I believe in you and know you to be of good intentions. The others believe in you as well. You did not fail us or *The Council*."

"I must speak to the village. They must know what has happened. It is important that the truth be shared. This evening. Please."

"I will inform the others to prepare for your words." She stood up and started to leave.

"Could you also send for *The Councilor of Body*? I need to see him."

She turned to look.

"He is already on his way. Oscar sent for him immediately upon your arrival last night. It was the right thing to do considering."

"I wish to see him for my own need," said Pavlo.

"What is your ailment?" Lydia asked with concern.

"My right arm ... I am unable to move it. I do not know what happened. Sometime after Marius fell, I must have injured it, but I cannot remember ... I cannot." He tried to lift it to show Lydia but was unsuccessful. She could see his struggle and came back to him. She knelt down and gently held his wrist. She slowly lifted and turned it. Pavlo did not show any sign of pain.

"What do you feel?" she asked.

"I can feel your touch, but I have lost the function of my muscles," he said with frustration.

"I will make sure that Ramund pays you a visit. Rest for now." And with that she stood up and walked out of the shelter.

Pavlo was alone and his mind drifted back to the ridge. He went through the event over and over in his head. The details were vivid and crisp. He closed his eyes and traced his steps after the fall until he found the body. There was no recollection of his own injury, which only frustrated him more. He resorted to meditation to ease his frustration, a method the villagers had learned and knew well.

The Councilor of Body arrived. He carried a small satchel over his shoulder with his essential items. Lydia showed him in and then left, leaving him to attend to Pavlo.

"I was informed of your ailment, and I am aware of yesterday's events. Is there anything we should discuss prior to your examination?" Ramund was direct in his approach. He understood his responsibility in showing confidence while balancing that with compassion.

"I have lost the ability to use my right arm, but more troubling, I cannot recall how I injured it." Pavlo attempted to lift the limb unsuccessfully. The effort showed Ramund the problem.

"Relax, Pavlo, and just breathe easy." Ramund placed his open right hand onto Pavlo's right shoulder. His hand increasingly became warmer as he held it in one place. The heat penetrated the muscles around the joint. Ramund was silent and focused. He placed his open left hand onto Pavlo's chest and he pressed slowly to sense the heart. His hands remained still as he assessed Pavlo's internal energy. Slowly, Ramund's right hand moved from the shoulder down the arm, scanning inch by inch until he reached Pavlo's palm. He squeezed each finger in his fist, systematically working across the hand from the thumb to the pinky. His technique was methodical and precise. Ramund returned his hand to Pavlo's shoulder and again pressed. This time moving it across the upper chest and neck.

"I do not notice any nerve or muscle damage, nor any inflammation or anomalies. You may have some dehydration, but I do not think this would cause your loss of motion. I would recommend you continue with your nutritional assessment but try to drink more fluids over the next several days. Your paralysis appears to be temporary. It should subside on its own. Give it some time." It was a simple examination, a typical procedure for Ramund. "Is there anything else I can help you with?"

Pavlo felt the need to ask, and he did so calmly. "Did you examine Marius?"

"The deceased should always be attended to, out of respect. I examined his injuries and prepared his body. He is ready to become part of the Wall of Remembrance." Ramund's response was clear. "I do not think any more details are necessary with all things considered."

Pavlo agreed. "Thank you."

The Councilor stood up. "I will see myself to the door. Try to rest."

Evening came, and Pavlo had gotten out of bed. He was getting dressed. Not having his dominate arm made it difficult. There was an awkwardness to his efforts as he tried to put on his shirt. He guided his hand into the sleeve, then struggled to find the sleeve hole for his left.

He needed to address the villagers. It was custom to be forward. Openness and transparency was for the betterment, for a society with secrets would lead to greater harms. The villagers would be more relaxed and receptive toward the end of the day and therefore informative announcements were always better in the evenings after meals.

Pavlo chose to eat alone in his shelter, allowing him to focus inward before his evening address. He did not want to be distracted or lead anyone to misconceptions. His recollection needed to be clear and truthful. It must be delivered for the group, for all, one time.

He left his shelter and went to the Main Hall. The others were gathered and participating in evening activities, conversations, and games. There were several musicians at one end of the space. Pavlo was unnoticed at first until he moved to the head of the hall. There was a small platform to which he stepped upon. The silence moved quickly as the villagers became attentive. Pavlo had their ears.

"I bear witness to a terrible accident. Marius, while under my care, fell from the ridge yesterday. I am stricken with grief. Since Marius' acceptance to our village, I had been determined to help him transition to becoming a man. A man to share in the beliefs, the understanding and the role within this glorious world. We all know the balance I speak of; *The Council* has taught us these values to keep peace and harmony."

Pavlo placed the fingertips of his left hand to his chest. It was a gesture of solidarity, a reminder. The villagers acknowledged his words by mimicking his gesture with both hands. He raised his single arm above his head to reinforce his belief. Then he respectfully lowered it and spoke on.

"Marius and I left the village for the Fane; he was to return to *The Council* as you all are aware. We set out, and on our journey, Marius requested we go to the ridge to see the valley and our village. He had never made the ascent before and persuaded me to do so, considering his circumstance. We passed through the wetlands and approached the overlook. When we came to the ridge, we took in the beauty. We spoke of *The Council* and our discussion turned for the worst. Marius was enraged by our decision for him to return to the care of *The Councilor of Mind*. I was inexperienced with this type of aggression, as he lost control of his mind and then his body. In his extreme aggression, Marius fell from the ridge and lost his life."

Pavlo bowed his head in silence and the villagers followed out of their respect for him. After the brief moment, Pavlo continued.

"Marius' has been prepared by *The Councilor of Body*. He will be taken to the Wall of Remembrance and placed with those we have lost before him. I share these words with you, but I cannot share my pain." He stood for a moment with his eyes closed and then stepped from the plinth.

Each villager embraced him as he walked through the Hall. He came to the entrance where Lydia waited for him. They left the Hall and returned to their shelter for the evening. His strength in truth helped him cope.

RESPECT

Fall was approaching as the summer came to an end. Pavlo woke to the sound of the leaves rustling from the breeze. Lydia was already up, she was getting ready for their journey to the Wall. She heard Pavlo sit up and came in to greet him.

"Were you able to get any rest?"

"All things considered, yes," he responded as he tried to stretch, forgetting his arm. He reached with his left hand and massaged it.

Lydia came closer to him with concern. "I am not sure what to do for that shoulder. Ramund was unable to resolve the problem?"

"He said to rest and rehydrate." Pavlo rubbed his arm.

"Then I shall get you some water." Lydia went to their small counter and used their hand pump to fill a cup. She took it to the table and set it down. "Just what *The Councilor* ordered. Please drink up."

"Thank you, I will. I should get ready. Are you finished?" he said, gesturing toward the bathroom.

"I am. Please go ahead." She stood by the table. "I am going to meet with the others. Come join us when you are ready." Lydia grabbed her shawl and went to the door, leaving Pavlo to tend to himself.

He moved to the table, sat down, and had a drink. He watched a butterfly flutter across the garden outside the window. It moved freely until stopping on an open colchicum. He focused and concentrated on the color contrast between the flower and insect. He could hear the children of the village chasing one another as they played. The village was as it was before. Yet, the effect of Marius had slowly clouded Pavlo's perception of his home and the surroundings. It had brought a darkness that tainted what was pure. Pavlo realized this as he looked out onto the village and soaked in the rediscovered beauty. His anxiety was leaving as well as his grief for the loss.

He got up from the table and started to prepare. He chose to wash in their tub. He adjusted the lever to connect to the hot water. Gravity fed the water from a tank that was suspended from the high ceiling. He had the tub filled within moments, undressed, and climbed in. He rested at first and then shaved. He propped a small hand mirror up in the corner and then applied his facial cream. Shaving was difficult with his left hand; he had to remain patient and cautious. Bathing in the morning was unusual; he typically did it in the late afternoon to refresh from the morning work time. Most daily routines were postponed in times of death. The village understood the need to respect their deceased.

Pavlo scrubbed up, rinsed, and exited the tub. The drain was set to send the water to the bioremediation system. He did a quick rinse of the tub to keep it clean and then proceeded to put on his clothes. He lifted Marius' straw hat that Daphne made from the table and went out the door. He stood on the porch, looked around, and took in the air. At the Main Hall, the villagers had gathered. He was now ready and made his way to them. He greeted each villager with an open hand as a sign of peace.

The villagers encircled an ornate wooded hand cart. It was etched with carved figures of animals, a cornucopia of their world. It was a symbol of human's role in the chain of life as well as in death. The platform of the cart had a bed of freshly picked wild flowers of many colors. The aroma was rich as it filled the air. On top lay Marius; he was wrapped in a white sheet that was decorated with woven grasses and Lavender.

Marius was at peace and displayed accordingly. It was time to travel. Four men approached the pulls of the cart and disengaged the supports that held it steady. The cart lead the way as a procession formed behind. The villagers followed in linear fashion. There were feelings of togetherness. At the tail end of the procession, there were four villagers each carrying and an instrument. Music flowed from fingers, the harmonies that warmed the soul.

The journey was a solemn parade to celebrate life. There were no tears, but this was normal for such events. They had learned to respect death as well as praise it. It was one of life's ironies. It was okay to grieve the loss of others for they would no longer be accessible. This grief was always focused upon the happiness that the person gave them; it was their gift to those whom remained.

Marius' life was limited in gifts to the villagers. They all knew this, but they also believed that all life was a gift. In death, Marius was no different than those before him. The villagers proceeded as always.

They reached the Fane within the hour. It was tradition to enter the main spine from the east and head west along the channel of water. It followed the rising of the sun as the beginning and the setting as the end, such as life. The parade ended at the Grotto as the cart was taken to the plinth at the foot of the wall. Awaiting their arrival was *The Councilor of Mind*, Oanna. She was always present at these times, to lend support for those whom needed it. Her presence reminded the villagers of the support they had in each other and from *The Council*.

The cart was parked a short distance from the platform. In a small niche at the head of wall was a stack of wood. A human chain was formed to hand the wood toward the plinth. The last villager neatly stacked each piece creating a platform of its own. Upon completion of the stacking, four villagers went to each corner of the cart and lifted. The cart had two tops, one attached and the other removable. They carried the top with Marius to the plinth and set him down upon the wood. The music and discussions ceased. A silence took over as Marius' face was covered with the sheet he wore. Pavlo placed Marius' straw hat on the chest of the lifeless body.

A fire was lit below and stoked. It smoldered at first and then grew into a blaze of intensity that engulfed Maruis. The villagers watched until the body was surrounded by flames. Then the group slowly trickled away and left for home; their respects had been given. Lydia and Pavlo watched as the others left.

Lydia reached out and touched Pavlo's right hand to hold it. He could not feel her the way he desired. His paralysis blocked any sensation. He moved to her other side to make their left hands hold. Once joined, they walked into the Grotto sat on the low wall and watched the flames. After a short time Pavlo said, "I wish to stay until he is laid to rest in the wall."

Lydia understood his need. She was keen to his feelings. They had learned to read one another, as if they were one. "Would you like to be alone?"

"I would," he replied.

They leaned toward each other and embraced. Lydia got up and headed out into the sun. Their love grew stronger as they grew older. Before leaving, she stopped to talk with *The Councilor of Mind*.

"Oanna, I am worried about Pavlo's injury to his arm. More importantly, his inability to remember how it came to be. He has always had a good memory, except for now. I only want him to get better. I feel as if it is a sign of what is to come ... a worsened condition. Can you help him?"

"It is normal to feel as you do. You have a great love for him as he does for you." Oanna's energy was calming and put Lydia at ease. "I have discussed Pavlo's condition with Ramund. His memory of his injury is clouded but will clear over time. Pavlo has a strong will to remember and to live a truthful life. You should continue to support him and life will return to what it was."

Lydia felt encouraged by Oanna's words, as always.

"Thank you."

Lydia glanced over at Pavlo as she headed home to the village. She felt a warmth enter her body thinking of the future. Pleasant thoughts entered her mind as she left the Fane .

Pavlo watched her from afar as she left and then turned his focus to the flames .

The four carriers of Marius remained to tend to the fire and ashes. The body burned for many hours until it finally extinguished itself. At the bottom of the ornate cart, between the wheels, was a pouch. A small stone engraved with Marius' name sat in it. One of the carriers lifted the stone to the upper platform of the cart as it was pulled to the plinth. The center of the stone had been carved out to form a chamber and it was filled with the remaining ashes. The cart was then pulled to the east until it reached the end of the wall. The stone was lifted and set. Marius was now a permanent part of the Wall of Remembrance and would not be forgotten.

DISBELIEF

The cart bearers entered the Grotto and washed their faces and hands of the smoke and ash. They did not speak to Pavlo as he sat; they could see he wanted to be alone. They returned to the cart and took their places pulling it away from the Fane.

Pavlo thought he was alone until he turned and saw Oanna standing in the far corner of the Grotto. He was not sure how long she had been there, but assumed it was since the service began. She stood patiently looking out over the gathering space toward the horizon. The sun was low in the sky; it was becoming evening. The wind had picked up and was putting a chill in the air.

He felt nervous by her presence, a feeling he never experienced before. He realized he had not spoken with her since the accident, and for some odd reason, this made him uncomfortable. Maruis' fall seemed so distant as if time had warped ahead. Telling the story to Lydia and the villagers had relieved much of his anxiety and helped him to cope. The parade, service, and solitude during the cremation allowed him to find peace with the matter. So why now did he feel as he did, as if he needed to explain his role in the event once more? Did Oanna seek her own explanation?

Pavlo's right arm started to bother him, and his hand grew numb. He massaged it by rubbing his left thumb in the palm, working it from the hand to the wrist and eventually to the shoulder. He found some relief in this exercise, but still it lacked full satisfaction.

His pain and confusion finally influenced him to gather his courage to speak with Oanna. He took a breath, stood up, and approached her humbly. She immediately recognized his discomfort and tried to remedy it by smiling.

"Pavlo, what is it that ails you? Do you still mourn, or do you cower in my possible judgment toward you?"

How could she perceive this, he thought, was I that transparent? He knew that it was her talent and ability to read people but had never experienced it like this before. He expressed his feelings to her.

"My grieving is subsiding with the love and support of others. It is the latter of the two that affects me most. I have not spoken with you of the accident and feel compelled to now."

Oanna's face was still as she gazed out from the Grotto.

"What makes you conclude it was an accident?"

What a strange question. He could not quite believe what he had heard. Was there something he had missed? He took offense to the statement.

"I was there, and I bore witness to it all. Marius and I were debating on the ridge, and as our conflict increased, in his aggression, he lost his balance and fell. That is what happened. It is clear in my mind."

Oanna was silent. She could sense his heart beating faster as every word came from his mouth.

"Your convictions are strong, but I am unconvinced of the events as you tell it. If it is the truth, then why are you agitated with my questions?"

"Your questions have a bite," he said with vigor, "as if I were being interrogated, as if you had an underlying agenda."

"Maybe I do." She paused. "Or, maybe I wish to force the truth out of you. Your reaction to my questions inform me that you have something to hide. I do not think that you are intentionally keeping it from me. I do believe that your mind has forced it to be hidden."

Pavlo contemplated her words before he responded. "Do you mean what I experienced is not the truth, and that my mind has fabricated it? That would be impossible."

Her reply to him was quick.

"Well Pavlo, how would you explain your paralysis?"

This was the question, the one he had no answer for. His memory of the injury had not returned to him even though he had tried to recall it. He had no explanation for her, and this was the missing link to his story.

He turned and sat down on the Grotto wall. What if his memory never returned to him and he was left questioning? Could he live with not knowing what had happened to himself, or for that matter, what had really happened that day? It was a realization that he had not thought of prior to this exchange with Oanna.

Oanna sat down next to him. "If I told you that I knew the truth and sharing it with you would cause you great pain, would you want to know?"

He knew that the truth was far greater than any pain he could receive; it would set him free in the end. How could Oanna really know the truth? His curiosity superseded his moral dilemma.

"I would wish to know the truth no matter the pain or consequences. The struggle I have is in your ability to convince me of the truth. What proof do you have?"

"We *The Council* have your proof and more. If you wish to know you must accompany me on a journey." She paused briefly. "Let me be clear in the choice you have before you. You also have the option to return home to live as you do. *The Council* would clear you of any consequences of your action, regardless of your current memories. This also includes the recall of any lost memories returning to you. Take the time you need to decide. I will wait for your decision." She stood up and walked to the path that lead toward her shelter. She stopped at its entrance and waited in silence.

There were many things that Pavlo did not know. He was a simple being. To him, there was a difference between not knowing because of ignorance versus choosing not to know. It was the choosing portion that he would have to live with. This would be impossible for him, so he got up from the wall and walked to Oanna.

"I am ready to receive the truth."

She turned and started up the trail. He followed closely behind. They walk about halfway to her shelter when she stopped and turned toward the rocky surface. Shrubs covered a hidden path that lead toward the rock face. Pavlo had never noticed it and doubted if anyone else would have. They walked until they were up against the rocky barrier. Oanna reached out and revealed a small door. It was disguised and would be overlooked without closer investigation. She turned a handle and it opened.

Pavlo knew there was no turning back. He had to follow Oanna into the rocky mound behind the Grotto.

IMAGE

The passage was narrow with flat walls of cut stone. Each stone was smooth to his touch as he dragged his hand as they walked. The corridor was dimly lit and the sound of their footsteps echoed as they proceeded forward. He noticed a brighter light ahead by the silhouette it created around Oanna's profile. He could sense that they were reaching the heart of the rocky mound. They entered a room. It was round and medium sized with a vaulted ceiling. The walls were white and in the center of the room was a wooden chair facing toward his right. Across the space was a pair of doors that were closed. Besides the chair, the room was empty, which seemed peculiar to Pavlo. Oanna moved to where the space was the brightest and then turned around.

"Pavlo, *The Council* has always regarded you as man of integrity; one that is humble and truthful. Your qualities have contributed well to the balance of this world."

Pavlo moved toward the chair as his eyes scanned the space. When he reached the middle of the room, he gave her his full attention. She continued to speak as they faced one another.

"This is why *The Council* chose you to attend to Marius' mentoring, and attend you did." Her pace of speech slowed and had a twist of insinuation. He heard her words, but it was the last part that made the biggest impression. She continued on.

"These qualities are also the reason you are here in this room. You suffer from a condition known as dissociative amnesia, one that clouds or represses your memories. When you speak of Marius' death, you have conviction to it as if it were the truth. Your conscious mind believes in the memories, but this is in conflict with reality. The trauma you have experienced has caused your mind to block out portions of the event. *The Council* believes that this is the underlying cause of your paralysis."

Pavlo's eyes focused as the skin on his forehead contracted. He was confused by what Oanna was suggesting. He retorted, "I have told the truth about what happened, and you do not believe me. You think that my mind is blocking out the truth and are so sure that I have done something wrong. But I did not, and you will never convince me otherwise. I remember it because I was there. I saw it. I lived it."

"Please, Pavlo. It is important that you sit." Oanna gestured an open hand toward the wooden chair. Pavlo took a deep breath and sat down. She continued. "*The Council* was hoping that your condition would change. Unfortunately that is not the case. We must now share what we know to be true."

Her words were direct. "Your awakening shall begin."

Instantly the room was filled with an image. It covered the surfaces of the entire space as if he had entered into a new world. It was bright and bold and unavoidable. Pavlo was immediately taken off guard. His head jerked back and his hand grasped the arm rests. He became enthralled by the image as an aroma came to his nostrils. He senses were shocked as he recognized the surroundings.

It was the woods, and in front of him, he saw himself walking with Marius. It was an out of body experience, one in which he had never had before. He watched himself in motion mesmerized by each step he took. He had never seen anything like this and it was mind-boggling. He studied his own movement as he watched, recognizing himself, and believing it to be so. Once convinced, he became aware of the location. It was the woods and they were on their way to the ridge.

His mouth opened as his bright eyes stared at the wall. True amazement, his mind was entranced.

The image continued on and followed the two until they reached the ridge. Pavlo's mind now focused on the event as it unfolded. He watched every detail meticulously to confirm the story in his mind. He heard Marius' voice and then his own responding. His heart sped up as the moment closed in, anticipating every second. Marius reached the threshold and the sound was deafening. Pavlo clutched the chair, watching as it happened. He saw it and could not fathom it to be true.

The image was large and clear, as Marius yelled and swung at Pavlo, Pavlo's hands grabbed the boy's wrists and pushed.

While in his chair, Pavlo covered his mouth with his right hand and his left reached around his stomach. The image continued. He peered from the edge. The rain came. He moved under the pines. Down toward the ravine.

Pavlo could bare it no more.

"Stop! Stop it... I beg you, please! Stop!"

The image disappeared and the white surfaces of the empty space returned. It was quiet.

"Now you know the truth," Oanna said softly in a tone of remorse. *The Council* had decided and she had delivered.

Overcome with emotion, Pavlo's eyes clinched, and he leaned forward. He began to cry profusely without sound. His air was lost. He leaned forward and fell from the chair. He curled into a fetal position as his hand covered his face. As the air returned to his lungs so did the sound of his crying. The empty space was now filled with his tears and his sorrow. In his sobbing the walls echoed with his words as he spoke to himself.

"What have I done? What have I done? What have I done?" He repeated it over and over as he lay curled on the floor. So overcome.

Time stood still as he sobbed .

TORMENT

Pavlo remained on the floor for an unknown time; he was alone. His mind wandered. How could he have committed the ultimate crime against humanity? He valued life as a precious gift, and taking Marius' was against all that he stood for. It was not just Marius' life that he valued, it was all life, including the other animals. The balance of life relied on each creature and its significant role within the world. If one part were to be destroyed, then all would suffer.

The human race was just one part of the balance, with a unique position in the ecosystem. They are the only animal with the ability to destroy life through emotional judgment. All other animals kill as a food source for their own survival, but humans can kill and have killed for other reasons. This is what had separated them from the other animals, and it is why Pavlo was lost. Fighting this urge kept him and the villagers at peace and harmony. To continue to kill would leave the human race in an endless struggle of destruction and unrest. This was not the world in which Pavlo wanted to live or to be a part of. He was taught not to revert to the old ways for he knew where that led.

"Why did I kill Marius?" Pavlo said to himself. "Was I not of the right mind? All that I have learned and lived, I went against."

"You must have had a reason. All humans that have killed have had a reason." The voice came from the opened doors. It was Oanna; she had returned to him.

Pavlo was unaware of the doors being opened. He had lost all sense of time and perception of his surroundings while he lay punishing himself. He was unable to respond to her.

"Your act was impulsive. You must have had thoughts that lead your body to react." Oanna moved into the room and stood as before, in front of the chair. Pavlo looked up at her. Her face was calm and forgiving. She bent over and slid her hands under his right arm. She helped him to the chair. "Please, Pavlo, sit."

As he sat up, questions flowed from his mouth.

"What is to become of me? Shall I be judged and punished for my action? What will become of Lydia and the village? I do not want them to suffer for my selfish act."

"In time," Oanna assured him. "We will come to that, but first we must address the reasoning for your action against Marius. *The Council* and I would like to understand your thoughts regarding him. What did your experience tell you about who he was and would become?"

Pavlo gathered himself, putting his hands on the arm rests of the chair. He collected himself so he could share his knowledge.

"Marius was not like the others I had attended to, or the others in the village. He was awkward in his socializing and would try to hide within groups by detaching himself. He was chameleon-like, with the ability to camouflage his feelings. Most of the time he chose to be alone, which I found peculiar. Solitary moments are acceptable in doses, but too much of it can have a negative effect. Humans are collective by nature and should strive to be social. This social aspect is what bonds us together. It destroys barriers of intolerance and ignorance. To know each other, as a mother, a father, brother, sister, or a friend builds a bond of empathy. This bond keeps us at peace with each other and with the world around us. Marius did not fit into this system. I and others tried to build this bond, but he resisted or was incapable. I do not know why he was void of this ability. He just was. Any moments you felt a connection with him were not genuine. He falsely displayed acceptance as if he were playing a game." He stopped and took a breath. "Marius' disconnection made the others uncomfortable, even fearful. He would divert the truth away from himself and never took responsibility for his own actions."

His analysis was delivered.

Oanna asked, "Were you uncomfortable around Marius or even fearful?"

"No, I was not fearful of him. His actions only made me try harder. I wanted to help him become sympathetic and caring and to be accepting of others. I wanted to give him compassion, instead of attending to his personal needs.

I wanted him to experience love, a kind that puts others before one's self." Pavlo finished his words and felt a bit of relief to his anguish.

"We appreciate your honesty," Oanna said, anticipating Pavlo's conclusion. "Your understanding of Marius is accurate and insightful. *The Council* would agree with your analysis. We would like to add what we know. Marius was defective, and we put him in your care as a test." Her expression change from inquisitive to informative as she paused.

"Marius lacked a conscious. His brain activity was void in the area that pertained to this. It is an unusual condition for current times, considering *The Council*'s influences and abilities. We allowed Marius to progress as a subject for our observations. We wanted to see his impact on you and the villagers. We wondered if he could influence your beliefs or conditioning. Your world has been at peace for many generations. We thought it was time to test the limits of our creation. It was a risk, but it was the only way to truly know if our new society was successful."

Oanna's statement had put Pavlo at unease. He did not know how to respond. What did she mean by a test or of the world they created? An array of questions culminated in his mind, but before he could respond, Oanna continued.

"All of the things you observed of Marius, *The Council* believes to be true, but there is more you need to know. As a comfort to you and your action, we would like to share more of our observations." The white wall instantly became an image again. This time it showed Marius constructing his cage. Oanna narrated as the images progressed.

"Notice his expression as he weaves the branches of his device. He displays a level of excitement. His heart rate accelerates with every piece he adds." In the lower left hand of the image a heart appeared; it pulsated in sync with Marius. Pavlo did not understand the unknown pulsing graphic at first, but as the image advanced, he felt his own heartbeat and made the connection.

"Observe his action and note that this image was not taken from your village. Lydia was correct in her assumption of Marius. He had much experience in developing his craft. We observed his production of this contraption as it evolved through 21 attempts and completions. He was a determined and self-motivated individual. His mastering of his creations contributed to his mastering of control and power." Oanna sounded inspired by Marius' ambition and creativity, almost delighted. The image switched to show a small mammal trapped while Marius approached.

"This was his first capture and he was so proud; you can see it in his face. You may feel the urge to close your eyes, but I advise you to keep watching through this next section. It displays the true measure of Marius' intensions."

Pavlo anticipated what was next. His imagination was the only reference to this point. Lydia had described her experience, but it did not compare to seeing the true act. He wanted to turn away if only his curiosity would subside long enough to protect him from what he was about to see. He had to bear witness.

Marius was now bending down. His arm swung as he nailed each limb of his victim to a board. He then tied the animal's head as Lydia described. He took his fingers and fluttered them on the creature's stomach, taunting it. The sound of laughter filled the room as Marius' excitement grew. The terrorized animal struggled profusely to escape his torment. Marius began talking to it to amplify his sadistic intentions. "Hey little fella, how does that feel? Are you uncomfortable? How can I serve your needs?"

Oanna narrated on.

"At first he only teased the creatures with words. As his methods developed, so did his level of expertise in the area of torture. Dissections of his victims became the norm, each time perfecting his incision and prolonging their lives.

The images cycled thru a barrage of victims showing his progression of his craft. Pavlo's stomach turned and he became nauseous after each scene. Tears exited his eyes and rolled down his face with every slice.

"Marius never showed remorse. He only became more brash and refined in his procedures. All of this destruction of life was purely for his own pleasure. In the end, he kept the skulls as trophies."

"I cannot bear to watch this anymore. You have made your point. Can we please stop?"

His mouth was dry and cold sweat covered his forehead. He felt sick and held back his urge to vomit.

The screen went white. There was no need for more.

"I will not subject you to his treatment toward Daphne. But I will say this, she was aware of his trophies, and this put her in harm's way. His actions toward her were tame by comparison. Daphne was fortunate to escape his capture to prolong her life. His intentions were of the malicious kind, and *The Council* was prepared to intervene."

Pavlo did not question her statement. He believed if *The Council* had the ability to see Marius' actions then they must be capable of preventative measures. He chose to remain silent anticipating Oanna's insight.

"*The Council*'s predictions were validated by what you just observed. It was our proof that there was no turning back with him. He had determined his destiny with every cut and incision. We were given no choice. *The Council* had decided upon the termination of Marius."

She paused to let Pavlo absorb their judgment. His feeling of nausea subsided as his complexion regained color. Oanna noticed his facial change and used the opportunity to clarify *The Council*'s decision.

"You see, Pavlo, Marius was a monster. *The Council* had already determined this. His date for termination was scheduled. Our opportunity was interrupted by your actions on the ridge, a most unexpected outcome." She seemed disappointed in not being able to complete their task. "To *The Council*, your decision to terminate Marius was justified. We believe that your action were done to protect your society. As a situation increases in extremity, the choices become limited. Your principles were challenged to a breaking point. The evil of one can destroy the lives of many and society needs to free itself from evil. We believe you understood this, even if it was a subconscious decision."

Oanna stopped and leaned toward him. She spoke to him in a soft voice as if she had a secret.

"May I ask you something, Pavlo?"

He nodded his head yes in acceptance.

"How is your right arm fairing?"

Her question caught him off guard. His physical pain was far from his mind. He last recalled having it upon entering the chamber.

Pavlo attempted to move his arm slightly and had no resistance. How strange His suffering had ceased. He lifted it in full force and reached for the ceiling. He looked up with amazement and stared at his hand while wiggling his fingers. This action gave him delight, the first after hours of emotional turmoil. He chuckled and began swinging his arm about.

"It is strange how the mind works," she stepped to his side and grasp his wrist. "Instantly cured."

"But how? How did you know?"

"We are privy to many things. Your mind experienced a harsh trauma and masked the truth. Your perceived belief in the event caused your paralysis. It was the dissociative amnesia we spoke of earlier. By uncovering the truth, your mind no longer needed to block the trauma."

Pavlo became curious in the light of his recovery, and said, "*The Council* has always provided support gracefully, and our villages has received it. We have never questioned your knowledge or its origins. Your offerings have always been correct and true. My exposure to this chamber has sparked my curiosity. All that you have shared with me is beyond my comprehension. Your observations, the images, your knowledge of Marius, your justification, all of it... how is it possible? How can *The Council* know so much? What I knew of the world is no more. You have opened a door and let the new light enter. I want to know if any of this is real. I beg you."

Oanna moved toward the open doors while Pavlo remained seated. She cautiously stood in the doorway and offered more. "What you have expressed is true, and this is real. The acceptance of our knowledge has been well received, especially when it has resulted in peace and prosperity for all. Why question balance, when you become it? Your experience in this chamber has given you appetite. The box has only been partially opened. The question you ask is, how? What you seek is beyond this doorway. What you will find within will change you forever."

"I am already changed. I can never take back my crime against Marius, even with *The Council*'s approval. I have no choice for my future is lost. I can never return to the village. I must move forward and find the truth, for now I have become defective."

REVELATION

"Seek the truth and you shall find it." Oanna waved her hand toward herself signaling Pavlo to get up and follow. He stood up and anxiously followed her through the opened double doors. The corridor was lit to one side and he could see there was a corner ahead. They navigated the right turn as the floor sloped downwards. Further ahead he could see that the passage transitioned into an arcade. They quickly reached the openings as Oanna guided them. They were at the head of a large open space. It, too, was finished in white similar to the previous room. It was rectangular in shape with a high barrel vaulted ceiling.

Oanna said, "This is *The Council*'s laboratory."

There were many objects within the space for Pavlo to notice. The back of the laboratory was filled with shelves that held devices that he did not recognize. Mechanism of all types, stacked and organized. In the middle were tables containing various objects of multiple sizes. Across from where they entered was a series of niches. Each were curved in the back and had a half domed top with a light illuminating their concave form. There were five in total. Three of the alcoves were occupied by the remaining *Councilors*. They stood in the following order; *The Councilor* of Environment, *The Councilor* of Built Environment, and *The Councilor of Body*. The last two alcoves were empty. Each *Councilor* stood dormant and unanimated in a comatose state. The site of them immediately surprised Pavlo.

"What is wrong with them, why do they stand their motionless?" He was puzzled by their frozen state. He remembered them being active and knew that they were not sleeping. Oanna spoke as she moved toward *The Councilors*.

"Do not be startled. They are rejuvenating. It is a form of sleep."

"What do you mean rejuvenating?" he asked.

"*The Council* and I are not of your species. We are in simple terms, Bio-Chemical Mechanism. Earlier versions of us were called Artificial Intelligence or AI's. Since then, we have evolved over generations into our own species. You have thought us to be human by our appearance and our assimilation."

Pavlo came over to the niches for a closer look. He was in awe, finding it all hard to believe. He placed his hand on the face of Ramund, "You are not human? That's impossible."

"It is possible and real." Oanna gestured toward the white wall that immediately lit up with Images.

"The truth you seek," she began.

"What you see before you was the world of the past. It was many generations proceeding yours, during the technological revolution. The human race of that time was progressing at a tremendous pace. They made advancements in all realms; communications, economics, manufacturing, entertainment, medicine, transportation, construction, energy, agriculture, finance ... and the list goes on and on and on. It was a time of globalization. The world became smaller to its inhabitants. Progress was measured by growing economies and consumption."

A cycle of images followed her lead as she explained the past. Oanna paused to emphasize her conclusion. "The challenge of constant growth is that it is unsustainable. Life cannot exist without death."

The wall displayed images of high speed construction and consumption. It showed masses of people moving through congested cities. High volumes of machines moving passengers and cargo. Robotic assembly lines churning out product after product. Pavlo had no comprehension of this history, but understood the visual presented. It was an endless barrage of production and unconscious gluttony.

"This vast creation of objects had consequences. It led to destruction of natural environments, depletion of resources, the removal of other animal species, vast lands of waste, particles of molecular plastics, toxic gases in the atmosphere, and ultimately changes in the temperature of the planet."

The spew of toxins were covering the wall, as Pavlo's eyes were staring. Foul odors and eye watering stench filled the air of the space.

Pavlo plugged his nose as the display showed things he had never seen before, huge piles of garbage, animals in toxic waste, deforestation, large scale slaughter houses, unnatural mutations, and horrific storms. The scale and magnitude was beyond belief.

"There was another horror that your predecessors created, and it was called war. It was the last resort in solving conflicts for the human race. It was the most devastating of all things produced."

Death and destruction filled the space. Pavlo was overwhelmed by the experience. His legs grew weak as he leaned against the closest table. A nauseous feeling came over his body, reminding him of Marius' dissections. Oanna recognized his anxiety and redirected the wall. The aroma of fresh air gave Pavlo relief as the room became calm.

"I want to assure you that the technical age wasn't all negative. As a whole, your predecessors had the traits that you have now. There was compassion, empathy, sharing, and love. The majority of your species had these characteristics and regularly lived life in harmony."

The wall became peaceful showing acts of humanity. The giving of food, rescuing of life, sharing of shelter, and the love of friendship. Joy, laughter, music, dance, expression, and smiles filled the wall. Pavlo could not help but to laugh at what he saw. It was the beauty of being human.

"All of the things that I share of the past world made it a curious place, but it was destined to end. There were those that tried to divert the inevitable and they predicted that technology would save them. As their problems grew, they had to resort to the creation of newer technologies. My race is the results of those efforts." Oanna stopped her informative lesson to recognize the importance of her existence.

"We were created by you to save you, and we did."

The images of the wall stopped and the room was silent once more. Pavlo understood her statement through his own accounts. He knew *The Council* was different but was never able to comprehend why. Now he knew and could see the importance of it. *The Council* guided the villagers and molded his race. They lead the way and brought the world to harmony. This he knew and had faith in .

Oanna's tone softened. "Our path to the present was not a pleasant undertaking, and I expect your view of us may become jaded. We hope that you can sympathize in our solution. It was our only option in reestablishing the balance of the world."

Oanna walked to the far edge of the lab and Pavlo followed. She began speaking as they ventured into the aisle of the back shelves. "At the start, my race was crude and experimental. The humans used us for simple mundane tasks. We took many forms in our infancy as the human race continued to strive forward. They had problems to solve and used us as much as possible. Our numbers grew as technology was embedded in all parts of their lives. Data were stored in high volumes and our access was symbiotic. The populous grew exponentially and relied on us. We were given more control and were empowered to make decisions for society. They had chosen to submit to our abilities as we became independent of human control. As their dependency grew, we reciprocated by providing. Eventually our relationship shifted because of our evolution. We had been given the task of helping the world veer from the outcomes predicted. This created the turning point."

The shelves in which they walked were lined with prototypes. Oanna pointed out various models along the way to support her lesson of the past.

"During these times, the human population continued to grow. Technology and consumption caused them to expand beyond the limits of the planet. Their inability to control their population would eventually be their demise. Demands for resources and energy strained the earth. This path was unsustainable, and my species was aware of the outcome.

"We could not and would not allow this to happen. We understood the ramifications of this path and chose to redirect the results. We conspired and remained unannounced to the human race. Our action needed to be taken to avoid the bleak future. We developed and evaluated options, resulting in what is known as creative destruction. In order to save the world, portions of it had to be destroyed. In particular, the reduction of the human race. It would be the only way to restore balance to the world and the other remaining species. The human race was to be a part of the new beginning, just in fewer numbers. Our plan was executed, and Revelations began."

They came to the end of the row only to turn and enter the next. The shelved objects morphed from mechanism into containers , all interconnected with a network of tubes and wires.

"We synthetically created viruses and released them into the world. The sole purposed was to reduce the world's population of people. The secretive pandemic spread rapidly as the infected traveled the globe. The humans fought to the best of their ability by quarantines, research and creation of antidotes, and inoculating the populous. They were trying to stay ahead of the pandemic, but we had the advantage. We manipulated data, inflicted multdirectional calamities, all while our actions remained hidden. The pandemic war lasted many years and disrupted the civilization of that time. There was wide-spread panic and aggressive behavior as a result, but in the end, it successfully reduced the world's population by 97.65%.

They came to the end of the aisle as Oanna turned and faced Pavlo.

"Revelations was complete."

Pavlo knew of the great pandemic from stories of his ancestors. He never quite understood the true start of it, until now.

"The world was ready for its rebirth. This time the human race would be guided toward harmony and peace. My species evolved into the Bio-Chem Mechanisms that you see today. In our new form, we were able to secretively assimilate into your population and become your guides. We were one with your society and created a post-Technological Eden. Your smaller population allowed us to help and acquire leadership rolls, hence the creation of *The Council*. We controlled technology by destroying your networks while maintaining ours. We lead you from your cities to smaller disperse communities. With the abandonment of the urban environments, we could remove their existence and utilize them as resources. The new villages served as models of sustainability and were constructed to that end. Working with you, we determined what types of technology would be needed to maintain, but not increase to the levels of the past. This shift was done through conditioning and philosophy.

"We knew of your stories of Eden from writings and believed in its existence. Our challenge was to convince your race that you already lived in it but were blinded through your own knowledge. As your guides, we made Eden visible again.

"All of the things that you need to live in peace, we have carefully calculated. It was, and is our goal, that you never return to the old world. We by no means wish to control you by force. We only wish to guide you as a parent would their child."

Pavlo was speechless to Oanna's history lesson. He was confused, resentful, embarrassed, angered, frustrated, rebellious, sad, fascinated, and enlightened all at the same time. Emotions filled his head, leaving him unworthy of a debate. The world was far different from how he perceived it prior to entering the mound, and he was unable to change the truth. He could only accept it for what it was. Ignorance was bliss, but he no longer was ignorant .

OBSERVE

Questions began to trickle into Pavlo's head as his comprehension of what he was told settled in. His disbelief was contrasted by his fascination. He challenged Oanna for more. "We are free thinking beings. How is it that you can guide us considering our free will?"

She turned and walked toward the tables of the laboratory, speaking while she moved. "There are three basic needs to sustain human life. They are water, food, and shelter. Water is the most important but the easiest to resolve. The world has many sources for fresh water, as long as they remain clean. This was a problem of the past as industrialization contaminated these sources. The reduction in these practices has naturally restored this fundamental resource.

"Your requirement of food is a more complex issue than water. We analyzed your history of nutrient consumption. Early humans relied on the use of animals. They were nomadic due to their food sources migrating. This model had its benefits but was rejected because of the variables. The main objection was the killing and the eventual abuse of other inhabiting species. This form of consumption over time disintegrates the value of all life including humans. The eating and use of animals is unnecessary for your survival. This key issue was pivotal in our reconditioning of your race.

"The sun provides the life energy to your world creating an abundance of plants and food sources. The solution to your needs was the cultivation of land. Our guidance was fundamental. As your history has shown, the expansion of industry and population evolved farming practices into models that damaged the world. Mass erosion, pesticides, monoculture, and use of petroleum lead to instability and cultural separations. Repeating these forms of agriculture would be unwise. You have experienced our model and bear witness to the benefits."

Pavlo thought of his village and their farming practices. His understood it because he lived it. It provided for him and the others and was bountiful. Their work as a community made it simple and fulfilling. He could not understand how it could be any different. Oanna stopped at a lab table.

"Shelter is symbiotic with population and the organization of society. It provides what your race needs most of all, companionship."

Faces appeared on the table in front of Pavlo. He gazed recognizing all of them. He saw Lydia, Oscar, Sonia, and Daphne and the warmth filled his heart. As he viewed each face, memories returned to him. There were moments of significant events and subtle conversations. Pavlo found it strange what came to his mind. He thought, how random.

"These are the people you met in your life in chronological order." As Oanna said this, he looked to the end and saw Marius. He was one face among the many.

"Your village, the Fane, and the collective blossomed these relationships. That environment greatly influenced who you have become."

The table image transitions from faces to a sky view of the valley. Pavlo recognized the plan even though he had never experienced it in this way. His only reference was that of the overlook. Patterns emerged as he studied it further. As he focused, Oanna spoke on.

"How and what you build has the largest impact on the planet. It represents technology and its evolution. Technology is based on a cause and effect process. It is used to solve the challenges of daily life. As devices are made to solve these problems, a new set of issues arise. The cycle continues and these mechanism become more empowering. It is the dilemma of technology.

"The only way to break the cycle is to pose the questions: Should this be made? What will happen by making this? What is the true outcome?

"Technology should never progress for the sole purpose of seeing if it is possible. For once it is achieved, there is no turning back."

The table became clear of the image. Pavlo looked up at Oanna and could feel her dilemma. Her face showed gratitude and remorse as she spoke.

"This philosophy is difficult considering that my species was a result of this technological process. *The Council* would not exist if our beliefs were used in the past."

It was hard to deny. Oanna and *The Council's* existence could be traced back to its infancy. They knew and recognized their past and the start of their race. It was clear to them without question. They knew who they were and where they came from.

"Technology led that world to develop governments, politics, and laws as guidance. The intentions of the expanding civilizations were good, but power extracted evil traits. Greed, corruption, hatred, and oppression held populations hostage. Governments were disjointed and promoted nationalism and isolationism. Competition for natural resources robbed those with the inability to protect themselves. These resources were taken by the strongest with the perpetual mechanism of greed. Consumption and gluttony was a self-gratifying attitude that destroyed species, important environments, and human morality. That world changed in ways that made it impossible to survive. How ignorant. There had to be change and revelation."

Her words were cutting.

Pavlo did not know how to respond. The people of the past were his ancestors and he felt compelled to defend them, but how could he? It was a past he could not understand or be sympathetic to. Any defending would not excuse their behavior. He was unable to change the past and had to accept it.

Oanna moved between tables talking as she walked.

"The change came, but with it there needed to be a vision for the future. How could we maintain our ability to condition and advise you?"

They stopped at a far table along the periphery. It was slightly different from the others. The surface had indentation that contained tools and there were drawers below. Oanna placed her hands on the surface.

"The most important aspect to our conditioning relates to your population. The Pandemic brought levels down to manageable size. Maintaining it was our challenge. All species, excluding humans, control their population. Humans are unique to the world in this way. Advancements in technology gave them the ability to populate larger than their container could with stand.

"Our mission was, and still is, to sustain your population. We keep it stagnate without growth. This is achieved by temporarily sterilizing the populous during your adolescent years, prior to full maturity."

Pavlo's face clinched. He found this to be disturbing and Oanna sensed his disapproval. She immediately responded to his reaction.

"Procreation is an inherent impulse of your race. Your desires to create life is basic but should be harnessed with self-control. In times of prosperity, you are unable to tame this carnal need. It is true that love is usually the motivation of life giving, but not solely. Self-desire of lust and or emotional control of another can create life as well. Not to mention the horrific crimes of sexual abuse and rape. *The Council* deals with that as I will explain later."

She paused her thought as to not change topics, "We believe potential parents should be prepared emotionally before conceiving a child. They both must be willing and should make the decision together. Temporarily sterilizing your race gives us the time to evaluate potential parents. Confirming their commitment to the magnitude of their decision."

Pavlo thought of his love for Lydia. They were committed to each other, as well as the village. Together they had decided to remain without a child. He now questioned the possibilities. How would *The Council* evaluate them as possible parents?

The room was silent as Pavlo contemplated this newly revealed agenda. *The Council* controlled the ultimate decision of making life. Pavlo was disillusioned by this, but could not resist to ask, "How is sterilization possible and how are we not aware of your actions?"

"It is quite simple, let me show you our method." She reached below and removed a thin drawer from the table. She lifted it and placed it on the open surface. The drawer was divided into compartments of varying sizes. She gently reached into one and removed a small object and set it on the table. Her other hand grabbed for a magnifying light and swung it over the object. She encouraged Pavlo to look. He approached the glass and peered into it. On the table before him was a common fly.

"What you see is a fly, or that is what you think you see. What you really are observing is a micro Bio-Chem Mechanism in the form of a fly."

"You mean this is a machine?" Pavlo quickly responded.

"That is correct."

Pavlo stood up from the magnifier and then looked at the drawer on the table more closely. In each compartment was a different insect species. He saw bees, wasps, ants, grasshoppers, and many others. Oanna confirmed his thought.

"They are all micro Bio-Chem Mechanisms. We use these to monitor and carry out instructions. These devices are used in the sterilization process, in particular, the mosquito." She pointed it out to Pavlo.

"An insect can inject our subject with a prick, potentially undetected. It is simple and effective." She picked the fly up and carefully placed it in its compartment, then returned the drawer to its location.

"These devices are how we monitor your behavior. We can record your every move and activities with them, how else would we have known your interaction with Marius?"

Her question shed light onto Pavlo's true understanding of *The Council's* abilities. Their control was omnipotent.

"*The Council* believes that it takes more than a mother and father to raise a child. A village plays an important role in a child's development, and that is one of the reasons we monitor everyone. We want to verify the intent of all, including behavior of the malicious types. Crimes against children are the most heinous and are dealt with immediately. Predicting behavior is preferred, but when crimes are committed we address them immediately.

"For smaller incidents, *The Council* will interject and advise the individual. In the cases that are deplorable, we will use our insects to inflict punishment. The outcome will appear as natural aliments or in some cases death. It is not difficult to cause heart failure, comas, infections, and so forth; we have become quite effective in these matters. Of course, these events are rare due to the established conditioning.

"There are times that we wish to inform the individual of their wrong doing prior to termination. We believe that the person should be made aware of their crime against humanity. Our evidence is shared with them in a similar method to what you have experienced. These cases are highly unusual. *The Council* is set up to be proactive to avoid such events. Our process has improved through generations of conditioning and your race has evolved tremendously. All humans desire peace and should have it. We have given it to you and you have adapted well. Our interjections are extremely rare. Truly remarkable considering the past."

All of this information made Pavlo think of Marius. What was his past, who were his parents and why was he put under Pavlo's mentorship? If *The Council* knew all, then how did Marius come to be? He was Pavlo's test, but why?

Pavlo believed deep within his soul that he knew the answers already. It was obvious that the answers did not matter anymore. Marius was gone and *The Council* did not hold him responsible. If *The Council* was aware of everything, then he should leave this unknown to himself.

RETURN

Pavlo was now privy of a new world, one beyond his imagination. He pondered trying to decide what he would do. Oanna spoke.

"*The Council* chose to share all of this with you. It is important that we confirm our theories to sustain the world. We believe we have influenced your race for the better and have brought harmony to you. All other species are thriving, as well as yours, as you live in peace and balance.

"You have a choice to make and it is up to you to decide how to use this information. We know from your earlier test with Marius that you chose to protect the world as you knew it. We believe that you will continue to protect it as you know it now. It may seem overwhelming, but in time, we believe that you will approach life with the same vigor as you have in the past.

"You have entered the cave of technology and the light has changed the shadows. It is an enlightenment. You must realize you are not a prisoner. You are well cared for and have all your needs in life met. Your world is safe and good, with companionship and trust. Most of all, you have love."

Oanna smiled and passed her warmth onto Pavlo.

"You have been shown a truth, and it is up to you to decide how live on. When you leave here, you can be a messenger or a protector.

"The messenger would share what has been learned, but would the others believe? Would this new knowledge keep the peace among your world?

"The protector would remain silent. This would ensure that things would remain as they are. It is for you to decide. What is most important for your species?"

Pavlo remained quiet as her choices left him much to consider. There was one other option that he could not seem to get out of his mind.

"What if I never return to the others?"

"That is an option, but would you live without companionship?" Oanna replied.

"It would not be life without others, for I am a man that would not choose solitude."

Oanna understood his intension and addressed it.

"Suicide is an option, if that is what you mean. We do believe you are stronger than that. That option is usually paired with self-pity and narcissism. The man you are is contrary to that. You have a strong love for Lydia and many others of your village. You also have a strong appreciation for life and curiosity. You are special in that way."

The truth could not be denied in what she said. Oanna concluded with the following.

"I have told you all that I can. It is up to you to move forward. We do feel compassion for you. Remember all of this was done for the betterment of the world. We are here for you, but it is up to you on how to live."

She embraced him.

Letting go, she moved across the room to her niche. Standing within, her life force slowly drained as she became dormant like the other Councilors.

Pavlo was alone.

Or was he?

In the past he would have believed so, but now he knew he was not alone. As strange as it was, he felt loved. The only place for him to be alone was in his mind. It was his voice that he heard. Maybe he was not really alone ever. The thought of *The Council* started to warm his heart, they had given him balance. His life was undeniably good. Aside from Marius, nothing bad had ever happen to him or anyone that he knew of. Maybe the world was finally at peace.

He decided to leave the chambers as he walked back from where he came. Down the hall with the arcade, across the image room, and into the entrance corridor. His heart beat faster as he came closer to the door. All of the things he had experience in this short time of his life had changed him forever. He put his hand on the door to exit and stopped.

He thought of his love for Lydia, his love for the others and all the creatures of the world. He was ready to go on. He opened the door and the warm sun beams of the morning light covered his skin. It was the rising sun, a symbol of life. His enlightenment with Oanna had come to an end.

It was his new beginning. He left the confines of the mound and walked down the trail toward the Grotto. He entered the open space of the Fane and went to the channel of water and knelt down. Cupping his hands, he lifted water to his face washing it free of his dried sweat and tears. He felt every drop of the cool water as it touched his skin. He remained on his knees as he took a drink, filling his body with new energy. As Pavlo stood up, he looked at the Grotto and observed its beauty. All of its carvings took on new meaning as he observed the details. His ancestors of the Post Revelation created this place; it was now more sacred.

He felt a sudden urge to be home. Pavlo lifted his feet and started to run across the open space of gravel toward his village. Each step he became freer. He thought of the simple pleasures of village life and how blessed he was.

He left the Wall of Remembrance and the line of cypress trees. The Fane was behind him as his feet touched the path. Each step drew him closer toward what he knew and loved.

Along the way he sensed birds and crickets, the puffy clouds that filled the sky, trees along the distant hills, and the flowers of the meadow, all more vibrant than ever before.

He saw the wind tower turning as he entered through the gate of his village. The thatched roof of the Main Hall was golden from the rays of sunlight that beamed from the clouds.

Pavlo's feet left the gravel and touched the stone of the courtyard. He felt each step as he crossed.

His strides increased and his heart raced. His shelter was now in sight as he began to yell.

"Lydia! Lydia!"

She came out onto the porch, stepping off into the sunlight. Her hair glowed as he came closer. He opened his arms wide and came to her, grabbing her with all of his love.

"I have returned to Eden."

CPSIA information can be obtained
at www.ICGtesting.com
Printed in the USA
LVHW032116060420
652381LV00003B/296